UNMASK

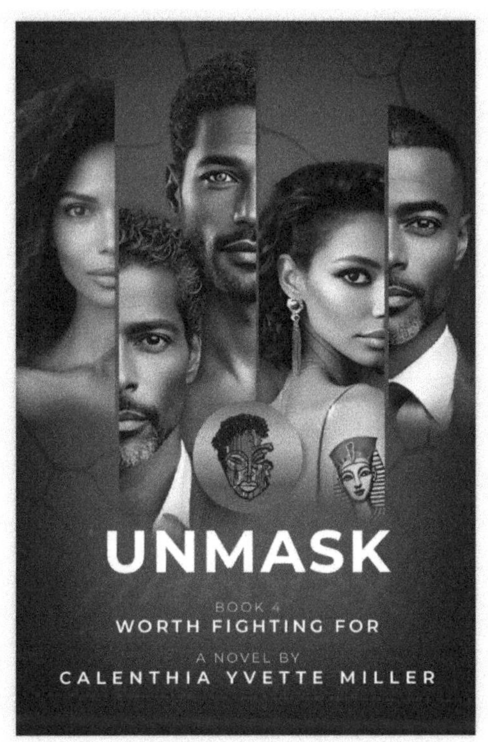

BOOK 4

WORTH FIGHTING FOR

A NOVEL BY

CALENTHIA YVETTE MILLER

UNMASK

BOOK 4

WORTH FIGHTING FOR

A NOVEL BY

CALENTHIA YVETTE MILLER

UNMASK Book 4: Worth Fighting For

Copyright © 2025 by Calenthia Yvette Miller

For information contact:

alurepublishingllc@gmail.com

www.alurepublishing.net

T: 919-391-8502

ISBN: 979-8-9902920-6-2

Paperback Publication Date: April 21, 2025

Illustration by Anthony L. Wardrett

DEDICATION

I owe a great deal of gratitude to Mr. Washington, my English professor at Malcolm X Community College. He was astute in identifying a diamond in the rough. He pushed me out of my comfort zone and recognized my writing abilities.

I am living out my dream thanks to his unwavering support and guidance.

TABLES OF CONTENTS

Prologue

Anya hugged Leah before leaving the hospital for the night. As she walked toward the elevator, Leah's question replayed like a broken record:

Are you and Royce okay?

Anya could not lie to herself—they were not okay, and she did not know if they ever would be.

As she waited for the elevator, Anya sensed Royce approaching. She recognized his confident gait and the distinct cologne he always wore. The scent invaded her space, making her nervous. They had not been in each other's presence for two days. Anya had slept in the guest room while Royce stayed in their shared bedroom. Anya missed him but could not move past the fact that he had been dishonest with her. She wanted to believe this was a terrible misunderstanding.

Royce was surprised to see Anya but relieved at the same time. He had been incredibly stressed for the past two days, as they had stopped talking. The tension between them was palpable and felt like a heavy burden. After receiving the first paternity test results, they had promised to be honest with each other. Royce feared losing Anya but also needed to know if Mia was his daughter.

As he approached Anya at the elevator, Royce could sense the same tension he had felt at home. Being an attorney, he was trained to observe people's body language and facial expressions—and he knew Anya well.

She stood rigidly, her arms crossed tightly over her chest, staring intently at the illuminated numbers above the elevator doors. The lines etched above her full, beautiful lips betrayed a hint of strain or perhaps frustration. Royce knew this was not the woman he had fallen in love with.

He stopped close to her, careful to give her some space. "I will be there by tomorrow to get some of my things." Anya nodded but did not look at him.

"Are you going to say anything?" Royce asked gently.

"No; everything that needs to be said has been," Anya replied.

As they went their separate ways, Royce thought about Mr. Overton's reassuring words: *Whatever you are going through, this too shall pass. Trust in the process; your time to love again is coming.*

Chapter 1

LOST

After leaving the hospital, Anya made her way to the parking lot, where she sat in her car, staring out the window. She did not want to go home just yet. While sitting there, she noticed Royce emerge from the hospital doors and walk toward his car. She watched as he opened the door, settled into the driver's seat, and started the engine. Her heart sank as she saw him drive away. The thought of him packing his things and leaving was too much for her to bear.

Anya needed to make sense of everything. Where had things gone wrong? Had she expected Royce to react differently? Did she expect something from him that she knew she could not reciprocate? The one thing Anya was sure of was that she loved Royce, but she was unsure if love was enough.

Suddenly the phone rang, pulling her from her thoughts. It was Terri, her realtor, on the other end.

"Hi, Anya. I'm sorry I missed your call."

"No worries, Terri," Anya replied.

"You are scheduled to tour the property on Saturday morning at nine. A real estate investor has shown interest in it."

"How much interest?" Anya inquired.

"High enough to call for an offer above the asking price," Terri said. "If you are interested after viewing the property, you should make an offer."

"What is the asking price?"

"Six hundred thousand, which is low for the area," Terri said. "Is there a reason it's so low?" Anya asked.

"It requires some cosmetic enhancements, and the roof and electrical wiring need to be replaced."

"How much would the repairs cost if I purchase the building?"

"You'd be charged an additional $250 thousand to $300 thousand on top of the asking price."

Anya let out a heavy sigh. Her budget for this purchase could not exceed

$825 thousand. "Terri, can we negotiate the asking price?"

Terri laughed. "There is always room for negotiation. Because the property has been on the market for over ninety days, we have some leverage to negotiate the asking price. I will do my best to get you within your budget," she said.

"I'm glad to hear that," Anya said. "I'll be arriving in Miami on Friday. Could you please text me the address of the property? I'll meet you there on Saturday."

Terri replied, "No need for that. I'll have a car pick you up from your hotel and bring you to the property. Where are you staying?"

"I'm staying at an Airbnb in the Arts District, and I don't mind walking to the building."

"Okay, I'll text you the address then," Terri said before they ended the call.

As Anya drove past her house, she hoped to find a place to unwind and reflect on the past few weeks. However, going home would only remind her of Royce, so she headed to the office instead. There, she planned to work on some accounts and review the numerous emails in her inbox.

Upon entering the building with her key fob, Anya walked to the elevator.

A chill went down her spine as though she was being watched. She quickly surveyed the area but saw no one nearby, though she could hear someone walking down the corridor. Reaching inside her coat pocket, she grasped the palm-sized mace she kept with her.

She looked up at the numbers above the elevator and saw it was currently on the sixth floor, the same floor she was heading to. Anya found that to be odd. Waving her key fob over the magnetic strip, she tried signaling the elevator a few more times. But it remained on the sixth floor, unmoving.

"My apologies," said a man's voice. Anya spun around, her hand tightly gripping the mace in her pocket. "We weren't expecting anyone in the building tonight, as the elevator is down due to repairs."

"How long will the repairs take?" Anya asked.

"They should be completed within the hour," he replied.

"Alright, I'll take the stairs. I could use the exercise," Anya said, trying to sound enthusiastic.

As she climbed the stairs, Anya realized she had made a mistake. She had to pause and catch her breath on the third floor! She chuckled and made a mental note to hit the gym when she returned from Miami.

Anya wiped the sweat from her brow as she turned the door handle to the office. The moonlight illuminated the entrance to the receptionist area. She walked to the break room and retrieved a bottle of water and something to snack on.

Then she headed toward her office, memories flooding her mind.

She recalled the first day she had entered the space and immediately knew this was where she was supposed to be. The space she would create generational wealth for her children and their children. Anya's heart began to ache as she also remembered the sadness of finding her best friend unresponsive on the floor, the space where she would never bring her dad. The space she sought refuge in after she had been violated. But it was also the space where she had found her soulmate.

Anya focused on why she had come and turned on the lights and computer in her office. As expected, there were multiple unread emails, some of which were marked as important. She dived in, answering emails and taking care of some administrative tasks.

Taking a break later to stretch and stifle a yawn, she realized it was already four a.m. Anya gathered her belongings, turned off the computer and lights, left a note on Stacie's desk requesting a Zoom link for Abbey's meeting today, and headed home.

When she arrived, Anya immediately began packing her bags. Unsure how long she would stay in Miami, she packed everything she might need for an extended stay. By seven, she was done. She had plenty of time to shower, prepare something to eat, and visit Leah before her flight at two this afternoon.

She decided to have an Uber take her to the hospital and then to the airport. The driver arrived just before nine. The ride to the hospital was quiet. Vivid memories of her last ride came rushing back. Why had these pivotal events in her life started to resurface now? Was it her subconscious trying to reveal something to her? Anya pushed the thoughts out of her mind.

The driver pulled up to the hospital's entrance, opened the rear door, and helped Anya out. He said he would return at eleven thirty to take her to the airport.

Anya was excited to spend some time with Leah. When she entered the room, Leah stood facing the window, looking out. Anya wondered what was going on in her mind. So many things had happened to her the past month.

"I know you are ready to go home," Anya said. Leah turned around with tears in her eyes.

Without hesitation, Anya rushed to Leah's side, consoling her.

After shedding some tears and sitting in silence for a while, Leah finally spoke up. "When I came to the hospital, my only concern was myself. But now, my focus has shifted to include this baby. I can't even begin to describe how protective I feel toward this little one. Seeing them on the ultrasound screen made all my doubts vanish, and I instantly fell in love. I finally understand what my mother meant when she said, 'The joy of motherhood is priceless.' "

Anya was thrilled for Leah and Bryce and did not doubt they would be wonderful parents. She spent the remaining time with Leah, discussing the next steps once she was released. Anya was relieved that Royce was not mentioned during their conversation, as she did not have the energy to explain their complicated situation.

* * *

Just before boarding her flight, Anya met with Abbey's team to discuss the legal aspects of their potential partnership. However, she sensed hesitation from their chief financial officer, Craig Thompson. Craig's concerns were understandable as this partnership had a lot at stake. After deciding to establish a satellite office in Miami, Anya had reached out to her financial advisor to forecast this venture's possible profit and loss. Fully aware that new businesses typically face challenges in the first three years, Anya was confident that their reputations would help circulate their names and pave the way for a successful venture.

Anya settled into her seat, inserted her earbuds, and reclined the seat as the plane reached its cruising altitude. She closed her eyes and relaxed to the smooth sounds of her favorite music artists.

Next stop—Miami!

Chapter 2

DRIVEN

Sebastián and Alex took cover at the top of the catwalk near the door and cautiously entered the vestibule. They could hear talking from the lower deck of the boat. Alex motioned that she would take the stairs on the far end while Sebastián took the stairs on the opposite end. Several minutes later, gunshots were heard again. Mr. Baxter called out for their status, but neither one responded.

Both Alex and Sebastián had direct sight of the shooter and hostage whom he had at gunpoint. They both proceeded with extreme caution. Surveying the area for any other presumed threat, Sebastián entered the room. His instinct told him to pay close attention to where Alex was.

Alex entered the room seconds after Sebastián. The shooter had his back against the wall, using the hostage as a human shield. He immediately yelled, "If you come any closer, she will be leaving here in a body bag!"

Sebastián noticed a red beam aimed at Alex. He fired several rounds but was unsure if he hit the target.

A warm, sticky substance began to pool seconds after the heat of a bullet pierced the lower edge of his bulletproof vest. There was no time to panic, only to react. Immediately aiming, he shot the suspect in the forearm and left shoulder, causing the firearm to be dislodged from his hand as he collapsed to the ground. The hostage, unharmed, ran out of the room.

After subduing the shooter, Alex barked into the radio, "Agent is down; we need a bus now! The suspect is in custody and requires medical attention as well."

Crouching down before Sebastián, Alex applied pressure to what appeared to be multiple gunshot wounds. She could see that he had lost a significant amount of blood and was losing consciousness.

"Hey, mate, you cannot fall asleep. You owe me another sightseeing tour of France." Sebastián smiled and said, "We have a date."

Mr. Baxter was the first to arrive. Lugo, Rex, and Tess followed him. Mr. Baxter ordered the team to sweep the boat to ensure all passengers were accounted for.

Alex grew anxious as they waited for the emergency response team.

Sebastián was barely talking. Just as she was about to get an ETA on the ambulance, she could hear the sirens in the distance. Then Sebastián closed his eyes and stopped responding to her commands.

Mr. Baxter crouched beside Alex, checking Sebastián's pulse. He immediately began CPR and asked Alex to communicate over the radio that CPR was in progress. EMS arrived less than five minutes afterward and took over.

Both Alex and Mr. Baxter were visibly exhausted and covered in blood.

Sebastián was barely breathing as they loaded him into the ambulance. Mr. Baxter thanked Alex for her quick actions and asked that she ride in the ambulance with Sebastián to the hospital while he called his supervisor in the States.

Alex watched intently as the medics worked on Sebastián. By the time they arrived at de la Croix-Rousse Hospital, Sebastián had coded twice and was in grave condition. The medical team was waiting as the ambulance came into the bay. Alex overheard the EMT mention there was extensive internal bleeding and Sebastián needed to go directly into surgery.

Alex was escorted to the emergency department waiting area and was advised someone would come and talk with her shortly. The medic handed Alex the military dog tags Sebastián had been wearing around his neck. He reported that it had saved his life.

There was an indentation and traces of blood where the bullet had struck. Alex traced the words inscribed on it with her index finger. All she could think of was this soldier had served their country on the battlefield and now beyond the grave. How she wished she could thank them for protecting Sebastián.

What if he doesn't make it through surgery? His family would be devastated if they could not be here to say their goodbyes. *Stop it!* Alex scolded herself.

Sebastián would be fine because he was strong and a fighter.

Her thoughts strayed to her encounter with him at the hotel. Though it probably wasn't the time to think of Sebastián in that way, she could not suppress the vivid memories of his toned body, his beautiful, mysterious eyes, and his intoxicating touch . . . But she could only imagine now, as she knew this was going nowhere.

The minutes turned into hours as she waited for news. Alex was now in the surgical waiting room with Sebastián's team: Mr. Baxter, Tess, Lugo, and Rex. The room looked like a command center. Tess and Lugo offered to go to the café to get coffee and snacks for the team, knowing it would be a long night.

As the clock ticked past six in the morning, the door to the waiting room opened slowly, and two figures walked in. The first was a tall, slender woman with a stethoscope draped around her neck—she introduced herself as Doctor Martens. The second figure was a man, slightly shorter and stockier, with a weary look etched on his face. Doctor Martens introduced him as Doctor Billings, her colleague.

Doctor Martens's eyes looked tired, but her voice was calm and measured as she delivered the news they were all waiting for. She informed them that Sebastián was now out of surgery and in recovery, resting comfortably. She went on to explain that Sebastián had suffered a ruptured spleen, collapsed lung, and a laceration to his liver, and during the operation, a small fragment of the bullet lodged in his lower back was not removed. Her words hung in the air, heavy with meaning, as they all absorbed the news and tried to process what had happened.

When Mr. Baxter expressed his concern about the possibility of paralysis, Doctor Billings responded with an uncertain answer. He explained that only time could determine the extent of damage caused by the bullet, and they would have to wait for the sedation to wear off before assessing any potential paralysis. Doctor Billings assured Mr. Baxter that they would closely monitor the situation and provide updates as soon as possible.

Chapter 3

OPTIMISTIC

Royce arranged for his belongings to be picked up from Anya's house and his office, then delivered to his home. He couldn't go to the house—it was too painful. He and Anya had built some incredible memories there. It was where he had told her he loved her. The place where he had made love to her. It was going to be where they would raise their children, perhaps a boy. In his mind, those dreams of forever after were fading away.

He had spoken to Bryce earlier; he and Leah were safely home. The joy in his brother's voice melted his heart. His boasting about Leah made his heart ache for Anya, and even more so when he had talked about the baby. Bryce had also mentioned that their parents and their sister Logan planned to visit in a few weeks.

Royce needed to find something to do. He couldn't sit around doing nothing. His priority was to find out where Bria and Mia resided. When Royce last spoke with Bria, their conversation had not ended well. He vaguely remembered Bria mentioning that she had grown up with both her parents and her brother Kane. Perhaps she had moved there to be closer to family.

He called Chris and asked that he reach out to Bria's lawyer. To Royce's dismay, there was no viable address on file for her. Nothing made sense anymore. Royce understood her reason for leaving the state after the first paternity results, but why was she now requesting another test?

During their conversation Chris indicated there was evidence of specimen tampering when Royce had submitted his first sample. It was also confirmed that the private diagnostic clinic used Coventry as its outpatient laboratory site, and that Nate could conceive a child. Royce's heart sank when he heard this news.

There was a chance Mia may not be his daughter.

The anguish of reading the first results resurfaced, and Royce became sick to his stomach. Visions of his childhood emerged in his head. He felt intense love as he spent precious time with his parents and siblings. Then, the visions of Anya cradling Mia in her arms brought tears to his eyes. But Royce had no time to feel sorry for himself. He had to devise a plan to locate Mia and Bria and knew the first person he needed to ask.

The ride to the Tennessee federal prison gave Royce the time he needed to formulate the questions he wanted to ask Lucas. He called in a favor and had his name added to Lucas's approved visitor list. Royce arrived in Memphis just before nine that morning.

Lucas had no idea that Royce would be there today. He was under the impression he would be meeting with his attorney. Royce had not seen or spoken with Lucas since their last run-in at his office over a year ago. Once he was on the facility's grounds, Royce was required to pass through a metal detector and be searched for weapons, drugs, or alcohol. He was allowed to bring his briefcase, making it appear like he was Lucas's attorney.

Royce was escorted to a detention center attached to the central prison. The room was cold, and the cinder block walls were grey. In the center sat a steel table with two chairs on each side. Royce could hear the distinct sound of footsteps approaching the steel door. The door slowly opened, and Lucas came in. His expression told Royce that he was not expecting him. The guard removed the shackles affixed to his wrists but left the ones on his ankles.

Royce felt a deep hatred and malice when he saw Lucas's face. He had regarded Lucas as a brother once, sharing things with him that he never told Bryce. They had always sworn to be brothers over women, but that pact was broken when Royce had discovered that Lucas might be Mia's father.

"I had a feeling that you would be paying me a visit soon," Lucas said. "I thought it would be after the first paternity test."

Royce took a few deep breaths as he clenched his fists. He knew this was not the time or place to display such behavior. His goal was to find out where Bria and Mia lived.

"This entire situation would have been avoidable if you had not slept with Bria," Royce said, his voice steady but laced with resentment. He looked intently at Lucas. "I need to know if you know where Bria and Mia are."

Lucas hung his head, seemingly lost in thought for a few minutes. "Bria was always a very private person," he finally replied. "But I remember her talking about her childhood in California and how she dreamed of opening a store in the Valley."

He continued, "I never meant for this to happen, and I apologize. The times that I spent with Bria meant nothing. We were both drunk."

Royce shook his head in disgust and replied, "Is that supposed to make it better? Ease your conscience? Guess that explains why you threw her under the bus when it came time to save your ass. You have shown me who you indeed are. Here I thought you were my friend, my *brother*. What's the saying, 'Keep your friends close and your enemies closer'?"

Royce gathered his belongings and walked away. As he entered the hallway, Lucas yelled, "I pray that the baby is yours!"

It was not a consolation prize, but he prayed Mia was his, too.

Chapter 4

ALONE

Anya, an avid traveler, had always preferred the convenience of nonstop flights, mainly to avoid the discomfort and frustration of layovers. As she disembarked from the plane, she breathed in Florida's warm, humid air. The sun began to set, casting a warm golden glow over the terminal. She checked the time—five o'clock, right on schedule. Excited, Anya made her way to the baggage claim area to collect her luggage and begin her adventure in the Sunshine State.

As the Uber driver drove toward the Airbnb, the hustle and bustle of the city quickly faded away, and Anya was met with a tranquil environment. The scenic views of the Atlantic Ocean were breathtaking, with the sun setting in the distance, casting a warm orange glow on the water. It was as if time had slowed, and all of life's worries and anxieties had been left behind.

This trip marked a new beginning for Anya. As much as she wished things could be different, she knew she had to be realistic about her future with Royce.

The ride allowed her to reflect, and she could not help but feel a sense of calm wash over her.

They arrived at the Airbnb address, a high-rise building in the heart of *Miami's* Arts District. The building was an architectural masterpiece, with sleek lines and a modern design that embodied the city's spirit. The bellhop was already waiting at the entrance, and as soon as the car stopped, he opened the rear door and offered assistance.

"Good evening, madam. Welcome to the Historical Art Deco Penthouse and Suites. My name is Hans, and I will be your personal concierge during your stay." Anya was amazed to discover that this service was included in her reservation. "Nice to meet you, Hans. My name is Anya McMichael. It is a pleasure to make your acquaintance," she said.

Hans took care of her luggage while Anya paid the driver. He then opened the door for her to enter the lobby. The walls were adorned with striking modern artwork and sculptures, creating a sense of elegance and sophistication.

"Ms. McMichael, please follow me. I have already secured your check-in, and I can take you to your room," said Hans. He led Anya down a long corridor toward the elevator. As she walked, she could not help but admire the impressive artwork that decorated the walls. She stopped in her tracks when she spotted a portrait by Henry Ossawa Tanner titled *The Banjo Lesson* and Aaron Douglas's *Window Cleaning*. These artists' work had left a lasting impression on her since she saw them in her art class during her first year in college.

As Hans conversed with Anya, he could not help but notice the way her eyes lit up when they talked about fine art. He commented on her appreciation for it and started chatting about his admiration for the renowned artists of the past. "It's truly amazing," he said, "how some artists can express themselves in a way that captivates people for generations, even after they are no longer here to receive their accolades. It's a testament to their work's power and impact on the world." Anya nodded in agreement, lost in thought as she took in the beauty and timelessness of each portrait.

Anya and Hans took their time as they continued to admire the artwork and the sculptures. Eventually, they reached the elevator and stepped in. As the elevator ascended, they were met with a stunning view through the wall of windows surrounding them—the glittering cityscape sprawled before them. This breathtaking sight left Anya speechless.

The doors opened to a luxurious penthouse, and Anya was awed. The sheer opulence of the place made her home seem like a simple shack in comparison. The penthouse's panoramic views were breathtaking, offering a bird's-eye perspective of the entire city. Hans was the perfect host, taking Anya on a tour of the whole house. Each room was more impressive than the last, and Anya could not help but marvel at the sheer luxury of it all.

However, the primary bedroom was the pièce de résistance. The room boasted a spacious sitting area with plush sofas and chairs, ideal for relaxing and reflecting. At one end of the sitting area was a kitchenette, complete with a mini fridge and microwave. It was the perfect space for enjoying a midnight snack or morning coffee while taking in the breathtaking views of the city below.

As Hans prepared to leave, he thoughtfully gave Anya all the information she needed to reach him, including his personal cell number and a detailed schedule. He also handed her the passcode and key fob to the penthouse, ensuring she had twenty-four-hour access to all the amenities, including a private chef and driver. Hans bid Anya good evening with a warm smile.

This is heaven on earth, Anya thought to herself. But she was curious to know how much it was costing her, so she pulled her cell phone from her purse and texted Stacie.

(Anya) Hi, Stacie. I made it to Miami, and the accommodations are beautiful. Did you book the PENTHOUSE?

(Stacie) No, I booked the suite.

(Anya) OH MY GOD! There has been a mix-up. I am in the penthouse.

(Stacie) There is no mix-up. Royce changed the reservation as a surprise for you.

(Anya) Royce had no clue that I was taking this trip.

(Stacie) Anya, you had me make the reservation right before Leah was hospitalized. As you requested, I included Royce and his legal assistant in the email.

Anya stood there, stunned and unable to reply. The weight of disappointment was heavy on her heart. She had been looking forward to this moment for months, eagerly anticipating the chance to sit down with Royce and plan their future in Miami. But now that dream had been shattered, and she felt lost and alone. She could not shake the feeling that something important had been taken away. This was the life that she deserved.

Anya showered and unpacked her belongings. It was still early, so she opted to stroll through the Arts District instead of going to bed, as this would be her home away from home for an indefinite amount of time. The city had come alive since she arrived. The streets were filled with people of all ages and backgrounds—the sounds of laughter, chatter, and the clinking of glasses toasting the night ahead. The neon lights that illuminated the buildings glowed warmly over the bustling scene, making it all the more inviting.

Anya took her time walking through the crowds, taking in this bustling metropolis's sights and sounds. She saw couples holding hands and groups of friends huddled together, all lost in their conversations and laughter. She also saw street performers showcasing their talents, adding to the ambiance of the street.

The city's energy was palpable, and Anya could not help but feel a sense of awe and wonder as she immersed herself in the vibrant scene around her.

The delicious smells made Anya's stomach grumble, indicating it was time to eat. She approached Tia's Market Miami Beach. The market was a bustling hub of activity, with vendors lining the walls, each offering a unique and delicious culinary experience. From the freshly made sushi to the juicy burgers, there was something for everyone to enjoy. The environment, like outside, was vibrant, and the sights and sounds of the market added to the overall experience. To top it all off, the market also had an impressive cocktail bar, which was the perfect spot to relax and unwind.

Anya purchased the short rib tacos with extra fries and a frozen pina colada. The food was mouthwatering but did not compare to the beautiful couple she met while dining.

Their names were Ernest and Mildred, and they were in Miami to celebrate their wedding anniversary. Ernest shared with Anya that he had met Mildred as a teenager in the late fifties when interracial couples were not accepted in the South. They lost contact after going to college, but they later reconnected during a layover in Miami twenty years ago. Since then, they had made it a tradition to come back to Miami yearly to celebrate their anniversary. Their story moved Anya so much that she offered to buy their meal and a bottle of wine. She then said her goodbyes and left the market.

The walk back to the penthouse was refreshing. Anya reflected on her conversation with Ernest and Mildred, which made her think of her parents and their love story. The way Ernest had caressed Mildred's hand and gazed into her piercing grey eyes gave her butterflies. It also saddened her, but it was clear their love was pure and genuine. And perhaps she, too, would be able to experience it one day.

Anya entered her luxurious lodging thinking about the email Terri had sent right before she had boarded the plane. The attached documents contained photographs of the building's exterior and interior, as well as notes on the last repairs and inspections. Anya had learned that writing a letter to the owner providing a sincere reason for their purchase intentions could help persuade them to accept her offer. So she sat down and composed a letter. She read it several times before setting her alarm for six in the morning, indulging in another shower, and heading to bed.

Chapter 5

A MOTHER'S PRAYER

Ja'Nae received a call from her mother, who sounded upset. Mrs. Margaret informed her that Sebastián's supervisor had called to tell her Sebastián was injured and had been taken to a hospital in France. Ja'Nae's heart sank as she thought back to the time when she had received the call about Leo and the devastation of losing him. She couldn't help but feel overwhelmed with worry as she imagined the worst-case scenario. She quickly called Sebastián's phone, but there was no answer.

She immediately knew that something was wrong. Panic and anxiety began to set in. Ja'Nae called Ms. J., but she did not answer. She then called Artie and informed him of the news. Artie and Ja'Nae had become close since their first meeting. Artie was aware of Leo's death and the trauma that Ja'Nae had suffered, as well as the relationship between her and his nephew.

Ja'Nae contacted Sebastián's supervisor, who provided her with the details he had received from Mr. Baxter. He also gave her his number and the name of the hospital where Sebastián was being treated.

Ja'Nae decided to drive the five-plus hours to the hospital to check on him herself. The drive was filled with anxiety and fear, but she knew she had to stay strong for Sebastián. She arrived at the hospital after picking Artie up from the airport. Ja'Nae was informed that Mr. Baxter had left for home and would return later. However, Chief Inspector Wellington was waiting for her. The doctors told her Sebastián was stable and they would continue doing everything they could to help him recover. Ja'Nae was relieved to hear the news and grateful she could be there for Sebastián during this difficult time.

After speaking with Wellington, Ja'Nae and Artie were escorted to Sebastián's room, where he was heavily sedated. He looked just like Leo as he lay motionless with tubes coming from every orifice in his body. Ja'Nae held Sebastián's hand and whispered, "I love you and will be here until you wake up." Then she murmured, "I wish you were here, Leo."

The hours turned into days, but Ja'Nae stayed by Sebastián's bedside. Artie returned to London, and Daphanie took his place as Ja'Nae's support. Artie and their siblings promised to always be there for their sister, providing her with constant support and companionship.

Marisa, her partner, and Ocean had flown in from her assignment in Bangkok. By day six, Sebastián had regained consciousness and could sit in bed and eat without assistance.

Ja'Nae became acquainted with Sebastián's team, including Alex, during the time spent at the hospital. She intuitively knew their relationship was more than just partners on the case. At least, that is what it appeared to Ja'Nae. Sebastián had not mentioned her, but in some regard, she would not have expected him to share something like that with her. Again, she and Sebastián were still rebuilding their relationship.

Mrs. Margaret called daily to check on her grandson's progress. If it was not Mrs. Margaret, it was Ma and Pa Franklin. Their genuine love and concern kept Ja'Nae grounded and sane.

Doctor Martens, Sebastián's surgeon, stopped by to check on his progress.

She and Doctor Billings had consulted with an orthopedic surgeon who had reviewed the X-rays and was not concerned about the bullet fragment and its proximity to his spine. However, she did mention the bullet fragment could cause lead toxicity, which could lead to nonspecific symptoms that might appear years after the injury. As a result, Doctor Martens suggested regular lead screening to detect potential side effects like fatigue, abdominal pain, and memory loss.

Sebastián appeared to handle the news well. He had no questions for the doctors besides when he could leave the hospital. Doctor Martens recommended that he not lift anything heavy or fly for at least four more weeks. He still needed dressing changes every six to eight hours, and the drainage tube would be removed after discharge. She also encouraged him to walk more to reduce his pneumonia and pulmonary embolism risk. Doctor Martens stressed that he would be released by the end of the week as long as he followed these instructions.

Marisa had arranged for Sebastián to stay at a villa near the hospital. This would provide a short commute to his follow-up appointment to have the drainage tube removed. She and Ocean stayed until he was released on Saturday, fourteen days after his near-death experience. Sebastián's team, including Alex, was there when he was released. However, when asked about Mr. Baxter's whereabouts, she was told he had a family emergency he needed to attend to.

Ja'Nae remained by Sebastián's side until he convinced her to go home and get some much-needed rest. By then, Stuart and Artie had returned, and they could meet Ocean and Marisa before they returned to the States. The circumstances of the time spent with Sebastián were not ideal, but it allowed Ja'Nae to build memories with him, Ocean, and her siblings.

As Ja'Nae was gathering her belongings and placing them in the trunk of her vehicle, a black SUV pulled up a few feet from her. The driver got out and opened the rear door. Nothing could have prepared Ja'Nae for the shock of hearing the familiar voice from the passenger that emerged.

Chapter 6

PUZZLE PIECES

Chris was still trying to piece together the puzzle about Royce and Dominique. Earlier in the week, Royce had requested that he contact Bria's lawyer and verify her last known whereabouts. He had already talked with Lydia, who confirmed no viable address was on file.

In addition, Royce's sample was probably one of the specimens involved in the tampering at Coventry Outpatient Lab. Chris wondered whether the series of events was merely a coincidence or if there was a deeper connection. The urgency to find the underlying cause of this matter was mounting and Chris was desperate for an answer.

Joy knocked on the door. "Sorry to interrupt you, Mr. Calloway. This arrived for you by messenger." Joy was filling in temporarily while Loren was out on medical leave. Joy handed Chris an envelope and proceeded to walk away. The letter was addressed to him, but no sender's information was listed. Chris was suspicious but curious. He inspected the envelope for any identifying markings, but there was nothing—not even a postmark. Chris opened the letter, glaring at the contents as he read it several times before placing it face down on the desk. He abruptly stood up and approached Joy in the receptionist area.

"Mr. Calloway, is there something that you need?" "Yes, can you describe the person who left this letter?"

She tilted her head and answered, "He was about your height, had black low-cut hair, brown eyes, and wore glasses."

"Thanks, Joy." Her description was vague; the person could have been anyone. Chris went back to his office and reread the letter.

Chris,

Keep digging; you are on to something. Just know that many questions will be answered very soon.

He was unsure of the writer's intent but knew he was too close to stop. He gathered his belongings, including the mysterious letter. He asked Joy to reschedule all his afternoon appointments then left the building.

Chris pulled up to Lydia's office. He had called her and filled her in on the letter he had received. She was intrigued just as he was. But he had not told her his suspicions that Dominique may be involved.

Lydia read the letter several times before she spoke. "Chris, this letter was written by someone who knows you personally or professionally."

Chris looked puzzled. "What makes you think that?" he asked.

Lydia read the letter aloud before saying, "The writer refers to you by your name, but they could be just trying to confuse you . . ." She paused. "Besides Bria's case, are you working on anything that involves drug smuggling, multiple potential fathers, human trafficking, or lab tampering?"

Unbeknownst to her, Chris had a gut feeling that Dominique was hiding something critical about this case, whether personal or professional. "No," Chris told her. But he asked himself if he knew of anyone, besides Bria, who checked the boxes. The answer came back to Dominique.

Chris and Lydia ended their impromptu meeting and headed to a Caribbean restaurant near the office. Lydia insisted it had the best rasta pasta and oxtails she had ever tasted.

The Sunset Soul Bistro had an eclectic vibe that offered a variety of Caribbean and Southern dishes on the menu. Tonight, a local jazz band played as patrons waited to be seated. The host asked if they preferred to sit at the bar or wait for a table. Lydia and Chris decided the bar would be suitable for hanging out. As they settled in, the bartender approached them and handed over two menus.

He then asked them what they would like to drink. Lydia quickly responded, "Bourbon on the rocks," while Chris requested a bottle of beer to be served with a glass on the side. Chris was puzzled by those who drank straight from the bottle. It was the OCD in him.

Lydia scanned the menu before she looked up. "I think I'll have the jerk salmon, rice and peas, and a side of oxtails." Chris could not decide between Caribbean food and homemade comfort food. Ultimately, he chose smothered chicken, macaroni and cheese, cabbage, cornbread, and a side of jerk oxtails.

The food was incredible. From the presentation to the seasoning and buttery thickness of the cornbread, Chris thought of his mother and how he missed her homemade Sunday dinners. He enjoyed it so much that he placed an order to go and a double-stuffed brownie for dessert.

After eating their meal, Chris and Lydia stayed to listen to the band. The bartender handed Chris his order to go as he paid the tab. Lydia left the bartender a nice tip and thanked him for a beautiful dining experience. Chris chimed in with the same sentiments.

They walked to their cars and agreed to speak again early next week. Chris waited until Lydia was in her car and leaving the parking lot before pulling off.

Chapter 7

X MARKS THE SPOT

Royce was getting desperate after nearly two weeks of searching for Bria without any luck. It was as if she had vanished into thin air. He decided to enlist Ashton again, a private investigator he knew. Together, they combed through Bria's social media accounts and phone records, trying to find any clue that could lead them to her. It was tedious and time-consuming, but they were determined to find her. He hoped they would find her and Mia safe and sound so he could make things right.

Royce had not spoken to Anya since he saw her at the hospital, and he felt guilty because he desperately missed her. Deep down he knew Anya loved him, but he needed to uncover the truth. Overwhelmed by his search, Royce took a break and turned off his computer. He pushed away from the desk and leaned back in his double-stitched leather chair.

Closing his eyes, Royce tried to clear his mind, stop thinking, and have a minute of peace. After what felt like an eternity, Royce got up from the chair and went to the kitchen. He realized that he hadn't had a home-cooked meal in several weeks. Opening the fridge door, he faced a harsh reality: It was empty. Nothing but a half-filled bottle of Dr Pepper, leftover pizza from two nights ago, and a slice of New York cheesecake he had picked up on his way home last night.

Royce realized that, like the refrigerator, he was empty too. He needed to take inventory of the essential things that added value to his life. After clearing out the fridge, he made a grocery list. He then cleaned the kitchen, wiped the surfaces, and swept the floor.

By the time he finished cleaning the entire house, it was around two in the afternoon. He had just received his grocery order when his phone rang. The call was from an unknown number, so he decided to let it go to voicemail. A few minutes later, Royce listened to the message.

"Hi, Royce; it's me, Ma. I was calling to give you my new cell phone number. I lost my other phone and had to replace it. You don't need to call me back. Your father and I are at a church function in Myrtle Beach. I'll call when we return later in the week."

This was not the message he was expecting. Although he secretly wished it had been someone calling about Bria, deep down he longed to hear Anya's voice. Despite feeling a strong urge to call her, Royce knew it wasn't the right time. He saved his mom's number in his phone and began unpacking the groceries. Once he finished all his tasks, Royce took a shower and decided to go to the river—a place where he found solace.

He parked the car about five miles from the trail leading to the river. He retrieved his running shoes from the trunk of his vehicle and put them on before stretching and sprinting toward the river trail.

The refreshing breeze from the river made the run bearable. Royce's heart raced as he quickened his pace. Sweat dripped down his back and forehead.

Wiping the moisture from his face, he kept running. He had a sudden thought that he was on a journey of no return. He could see the river directly before him, but it seemed to get further away with every step.

Out of nowhere a sharp pain struck him in the upper right side of his chest. He gasped, stumbling to a halt. The pain felt as if a vise was tightening around his heart. Unable to stand, he fell to the ground. Royce's mind flashed back to when his father had been hospitalized. He pictured his mother sitting at the side of the bed, praying and asking God not to take him from their family.

He began to panic but remembered the exercise he and Anya would practice when she had a panic attack. Taking several long, cleansing breaths, Royce inhaled and exhaled, repeating to himself:

Focus. Do not panic. You have too much to live for. Focus. Do not panic. You have too much to live for. Focus. Do not panic. You have too much to live for.

Then, without warning, the skies opened up, and rain began to pour from the heavens above. But just as fast as the rain started, it quickly stopped. Royce glanced up and saw a rainbow in the distance. The pain in his chest subsided, and he slowly got up from the pavement.

Not sure what had just happened, Royce stood paralyzed by the fear of the unknown. Not knowing was what was keeping him trapped in this cage filled with stress and the inability to breathe.

At that moment, he knew he had to care for himself and love himself first.

He remembered a post he had recently seen on his social media feed. *Self-preservation is the key to survival.* Royce knew he was hanging on by a thread. He had too much to live for and was unwilling to let stress destroy it.

He walked the five miles back to his car at a steady pace, taking breaks when he needed to. When he finally reached his car, he took a long sip of water from the stainless-steel mug in the cup holder. The cool liquid was refreshing and quenched his thirst, though he could still feel his heart racing and his pulse pounding. He took a few more sips and reclined the seat, giving himself room to stretch and lowering his head to relax. After twenty minutes, his pulse and heart rate returned to normal. Royce made a mental note to call his physician in the morning to schedule an appointment.

Chapter 8

YOUR MOVE

Anya had submitted an offer for the property in the Arts District after receiving a quote for the renovation expense, but it had been two weeks, and she had not received any response. Terri informed her that several other offers had been made after hers, and it might take some time for the sellers to decide. She suggested that she look at different properties in the meantime. After viewing twenty properties in ten days, Anya was not impressed by any of them. She remained hopeful that she would find a property before she returned home.

Today was yet another beautiful day in Miami. Hans had given Anya several places within walking distance to visit. He boasted about the stunning street art, coffee shops, and virtual boat tours many tourists love. Anya ultimately decided to tour Wynwood and visit one of the art galleries and museums. She must admit Hans was correct—the street art was magnificent, the vibrant colors making the designs come alive.

Anya visited two prominent art galleries, one featuring the work of a local Impressionist artist, Thomasina Wagner. Picking up and reading Thomasina's bio card gave Anya a glimpse of her life. According to the card, Thomasina began painting when she was gifted water paint and a canvas for Christmas at age five. There was no doubt she had been born to do this. Each brushstroke in Thomasina's work glided effortlessly on the canvas, creating a stunning display of colors and artistry.

Anya walked every square inch of the gallery in amazement at each image she viewed. She was captivated by the beauty of *Marvel*, a painting depicting a young mother peering into a carriage at her sleeping babies. The gentleness of the mother's eyes moved Anya so much that she bought the painting.

Now the question was how she would transport it to the Airbnb. The curator assured her it could be delivered free of charge since it was only a few blocks away. She thanked her and headed back to the Airbnb.

As she entered through the revolving door, she thought she heard someone calling her name. She hesitated momentarily but then continued toward the elevator, eager to return to her penthouse. Just as she was about to access the elevator, she heard her name being called again. Anya turned and was shocked to see that it was Mildred, the lady she had met on the first day she arrived in Miami.

Anya greeted her with a warm embrace. "Hello, it's so good to see you again, Mrs. Mildred. Are you and Mr. Ernest staying here?" she asked.

Mildred replied, "We're here to meet some friends for dinner. You're welcome to join us if you don't have any plans."

Anya hesitated, not wanting to be the only one without a significant other. However, Mildred took charge and ushered Anya through the restaurant's double doors before she could refuse.

The restaurant's ambiance and décor were just as elegant as the rest of the hotel. The maître d' led them to an enclosed terrace overlooking a cascading waterfall reminiscent of Niagara Falls. The sound of the water was soothing, and the view was breathtaking. As Anya and Mildred entered the room, everyone erupted in a chorus of, "SURPRISE! HAPPY ANNIVERSARY!"

Mildred was filled with sheer surprise and began to cry. Ernest was there to wipe her tears away. Then he took her hand, and on one knee he said, "The first day I laid eyes on you, I knew you were the one. Due to events out of our control, we were forbidden to be together. But now we've been together for twenty years, and I want to spend the rest of my days with you. Will you marry me again, Mildred Louise Monroe?"

"Yes, I will," Mildred replied tearfully. As soon as she said yes, she was whisked away. A very well-groomed, handsome man got on the microphone and announced that this was not only an anniversary party but a wedding. All the guests were equally surprised by the announcement. Anya asked the gentleman onthe microphone what time the wedding would begin. He suggested that she be back within the hour, which would give her enough time to go shower and change.

Anya returned just in time to see Ernest walking toward the podium, where the minister, the groomsmen, and the bridesmaids stood. Ernest looked dapper in his sleek Italian double-breasted black tuxedo paired with a crisp white shirt and Oxford loafers.

The music began to play as Mildred was ushered down the aisle by whom Anya presumed were her sons. She appeared radiant in her peach crepe off-the-shoulder sheath gown with a side slit that revealed her toned legs. She walked steadily in gorgeous four-inch white feather heels with red bottoms. Her hair was pulled back in a bun, highlighting the diamond earrings and the matching diamond necklace that lay perfectly against her mocha skin.

Ernest and Mildred chose to recite their wedding vows from twenty years ago, leaving no dry eye in the room. Anya wept when Mildred said, "Although we were separated for those years, my love for you grew each day we were apart." The statement hit Anya hard—she missed Royce more each day. She yearned for a love like Ernest and Mildred's, not to mention her parents' four decades of marriage.

The wedding and reception were lavish, and the food was sinful. At the reception Anya had the opportunity to network and meet important people, such as Sasha and Mikal Wimbush, a brother and sister who owned a catering and home interior company. Also, Simeon Gray, who had spoken on the microphone earlier, was Mildred's nephew and owner of an architectural firm. The night was filled with excitement, and Anya had a wonderful time, feeling grateful that she had attended.

Anya returned to the penthouse after eleven, and she was exhausted mentally and physically. After showering, Anya contemplated whether to call Royce. It had been over two weeks since they last spoke or saw one another. She was fearful that he might not want to talk to her, especially after how things had ended at the hospital. In the end she lacked the courage and opted not to call.

Chapter 9

HEALING

Sebastián had been discharged from the hospital two weeks ago. Today he had an appointment to have the drainage tube removed and plans to meet with Mr.

Baxter and his team afterward. Alex agreed to take him to the satellite office in Lyon after his appointment. The support that Sebastián received during his recovery was undoubtedly heartfelt. He appreciated that Marisa had also arranged for him to stay at a villa close to the hospital. More importantly, the support from Ja'Nae, his aunts, uncles, and grandparents made recovery easier to manage. Just that morning he had received a call from Ocean and Ma and Pa Franklin asking when he would be returning home.

Alex and Sebastián had become much closer since his release. But he did not want to send her the wrong message about his intentions. The last thing he wanted was to mislead or hurt her. He knew they needed to talk about their relationship sooner rather than later since he would return to the States in less than two weeks.

* * *

Mr. Baxter was the first to greet Sebastián when he arrived at the office. He gave him a firm handshake and a warm embrace, saying, "Son, you gave us a scare, but we are happy you are on the road to recovery." Mr. Baxter calling him "son" made Sebastián think of how proud his father would be of him. The team assembled around the conference room table, and Mr. Baxter began to debrief them on the status of Operation Slaughter.

According to Mr. Baxter, Rex Slaughter and his accomplice were still in police custody awaiting extradition to the United States. He indicated that the female who was apprehended with Rex had been held against her will and was able to provide some valuable information to Interpol. The meeting lasted about two hours before Mr. Baxter allowed everyone to leave for the day. As Sebastián exited the room, Mr. Baxter asked to speak with him privately.

They took the elevator to the eighth floor and walked down the hall to an office just past the exit sign. Officers are trained to pay attention to details and their surroundings. And Sebastián indeed made a mental note of every detail.

"Please have a seat, Sebastián," Mr. Baxter said, motioning toward a chair. "I wanted to speak to you in private to discuss the incident. Specifically, I need to inform you that the accomplice who was shot during the incident was an undercover FBI agent named Josiah. For more than a year, he has been collaborating with us to connect Rex Slaughter to an international cartel that abducted the sister of one of our agents. Josiah provided information suggesting a mole in the Lyon office who is believed to be associated with Slaughter and knows the whereabouts of the agent's sister and other vital individuals in the cartel."

Sebastián was taken aback by this news. He pondered who the mole might be but refrained from jumping to conclusions. Mr. Baxter didn't seem inclined to reveal the individual's identity. Afterward, Mr. Baxter offered Sebastián a job with the agency, primarily involving communication with the Lyon field office and the United States. However, Sebastián needed time to consider the offer due to his responsibilities as a father.

He inquired about when he should give an answer, to which Mr. Baxter responded that they would allow Sebastián more time to recover and visit his family. In other words, the agency did not expect an immediate response.

However, he estimated they would need one from Sebastián within the next month, coinciding with Rex Slaughter's projected return to the States.

Mr. Baxter went on to explain why they wanted Sebastián to stay. He said he recognized his potential during this operation and believed Sebastián would be a valuable addition to the team. Sebastián felt honored by Mr. Baxter's high regard for his abilities as an officer. After wrapping up their meeting, Mr. Baxter escorted Sebastián downstairs, where he met Alex in the lobby. But the question remained: Who was the suspected mole in the office?

As Sebastián and Alex drove back to the villa, the car was filled with a heavy silence. Sebastián was consumed by his thoughts, contemplating Mr. Baxter's offer and its potential impact on his career and family. He also reflected on his relationship with Alex, hoping he did not unintentionally mislead or hurt her.

The silence was broken when Alex asked Sebastián if he needed to stop and pick up dinner before they reached the villa.

"No," Sebastián replied. "How about we go out for dinner instead? I haven't been out since being released from the hospital."

Alex suggested a delightful Mediterranean café near the villa.

"Could we swing by the villa first? I need to change," Sebastián requested.

As they entered the villa, Alex noticed blood on Sebastián's shirt where the drainage tube had been removed. The doctor had informed Sebastián that some blood might be present at the site and assured him it was normal. The doctor had also mentioned that the area might be tender, but the stitches would dissolve, and the incision would heal over time.

After a quick change, they set off for the café, which, as Alex had mentioned, was conveniently located within walking distance of the villa, nestled on a secluded side street. At first glance, the café appeared to be a residence, with its classic Mediterranean textured walls and stucco architectural design. The soaring ceilings in the foyer were supported by four pillars and several wood beams, while the plaster and stone walls were adorned with ceramic terra-cotta and wrought iron metalwork. The vibrant colors on every surface created a warm and inviting atmosphere.

The server seated them at a table in the back of the café, creating a romantic ambiance. Speaking with a heavy accent, she asked Alex, "Are you celebrating your anniversary with your husband?"

Alex blushed and quickly responded, "No, he's my colleague."

Sebastián was unsure what was said but thought the server mentioned an anniversary. Not wanting to embarrass Alex further, he kept his thoughts to himself. The server handed Sebastián the menu and paused as if she wanted to say something. A mischievous look appeared on her face before she walked away.

Sebastián could only imagine what she was thinking and how Alex would respond.

There was a brief silence as they gazed at their menus.

"So, what are you going to eat?" Sebastián asked Alex, who peered up from the menu and replied, "I'm not sure; what about you?"

Sebastián gently pulled the menu down to look at her and noticed that her face was colorless. Sebastián feared she might pass out. Wrapping his massive hand around her tiny wrist, he could feel her rapid heartbeat.

"Why do I make you so nervous?" Sebastián asked. "Have I said or done anything that makes you uncomfortable around me? If I have, that was never my intention."

"No," Alex replied, shaking her head. "You haven't said anything to make me feel that way."

"Then what is it?"

"I saw you die, saw the life leave your body, and heard your last words. At that moment, all I could think was that the bullet was meant for *me*. I saw the red beam of light aimed at me. I've replayed that scene in my head every day since it happened."

Sebastián also remembered the red beam aimed directly at Alex. And he recalled Mr. Baxter's words: *There's a mole in the office.*

Chapter 10

UNRESOLVED

Royce received a clean bill of health from his physician, but due to his family history of heart disease, he was referred to a cardiologist. As instructed, he arrived early for his 10:30 a.m. appointment with Doctor Willis. The new patient paperwork was extensive, and Royce struggled to answer many questions about his parents and grandparents. Consequently, he called his parents to get the answers.

The information Royce received about his family's medical history was enlightening, the most surprising being that his maternal great-grandfather had been biracial and had never known his biological parents. This meant his mother could not provide much history on her side, which made Royce want to dig deeper into his lineage.

The nurse called Royce's name and escorted him to the examination room. Once there, she introduced herself as Lani, gathered the paperwork, and took his vital signs. She noted that his blood pressure was slightly elevated and told him she would retake it to ensure accuracy. She asked him if he was nervous about today's medical visit.

"Well . . . I can't say I *like* going to the doctor," Royce replied. She nodded. "You may have white coat syndrome."

He gave her a puzzled look. "What's that?"

Lani explained, "It's when your blood pressure elevates in a clinical setting."

Royce had not heard of the term before but could see himself having it. He was no stranger to the clinical atmosphere of exam rooms and doctors' offices. It seemed as though he had spent a lifetime navigating through these settings.

However, everything had changed after Skylar's passing. This loss had a profound impact on him, shaping the way he approached healthcare for himself and his loved ones. It was one of the reasons why he was so vigilant about Anya's well- being, ensuring that she never missed a scheduled medical appointment.

As Doctor Willis entered the room, Royce could not help but be struck by her presence. She carried herself with poise and assurance that demanded attention. Her shoulder-length sandy brown hair was immaculately styled, falling just so upon the collar of her pristine white lab coat. Her knee-length floral-print dress complemented her professional demeanor, and the open-toed heels accentuated her toned calves. Every detail of her appearance underscored her confidence and expertise.

Doctor Willis greeted Royce with a warm handshake as she introduced herself. "So, tell me—what brings you in today?"

Royce proceeded to recount his incident at the river trail. As he spoke, Doctor Willis meticulously jotted down notes while carefully reviewing the paperwork Royce had filled out.

After a brief silence, she said, "Mr. Blackmon, I have carefully examined the results of your EKG, and I'm pleased to inform you that no abnormal findings were detected. Have you been under significant stress lately? Or have you experienced any traumatic incidents within the past six months to a year? These details will help me better understand your overall health and well-being."

Royce sighed heavily and replied, "I have."

"If it's too painful to speak about, I understand," Doctor Willis said empathetically.

He hesitated for a moment but then found himself opening up to the doctor about the emotional turmoil he had been going through, including the loss of Skylar, their unborn child, the paternity test, and his recent separation from Anya.

Doctor Willis looked at him with concern, her brows furrowed. "Mr.

Blackmon, it's clear that you are experiencing extreme stress. I strongly recommend that you consider seeking support from a grief counselor. The episode you recently experienced is a clear indication of your body's response to the many losses that you have not yet fully resolved. Addressing these unresolved issues is essential to effectively manage and cope with the stress you are facing. Ultimately, it could be detrimental to your health if you do not seek help."

Royce paused to process what he had just heard. Had he not fully grieved everything he had been going through? Was he hiding behind the grief?

Doctor Willis handed Royce a card for a grief counselor and scheduled an appointment for a stress echocardiogram a week from today. When Royce inquired about the test's necessity, Doctor Willis explained her intention to rule out cardiac conditions undetectable by the EKG.

Royce appreciated Doctor Willis's thorough care, as she left no stone unturned and no questions unanswered. Before leaving the office, Lani provided Royce with an after-visit summary that included information about his upcoming stress echocardiogram, a follow-up appointment with Doctor Willis, and the names of the grief counselors.

Royce knew that he had to follow through—the quality of his life depended on it.

Chapter 11

RANDOM

As Chris was getting ready to leave the office for the day, his phone suddenly rang. To his surprise, Dominique was on the other end of the line. They had not spoken since the last time they saw each other at the courthouse.

"Hello, this is Chris Calloway," he answered.

"Hi, Chris, this is Dominique Sanchez," she replied.

"Good evening, Dominique. What can I do for you?" he asked in a friendly tone.

"Can we meet somewhere to talk?" Dominique inquired, her voice sounding hesitant.

"And what do you wish to discuss? Your client?" Chris probed, curious about the unexpected call.

"Which client are you referring to?" Dominique responded, her tone becoming slightly more severe. "Mr. Calloway, I see that you are going to make this hard for me," she said, her frustration evident.

Chris rethought his approach. "When would you like to meet Ms. Sanchez?"

"Are you available today at seven?" she asked.

"I have a previous engagement. Can we meet on Monday at four in my office?"

"Okay, I'll be there," she said before hanging up.

Chris had tirelessly delved into Dominique's background, meticulously scrutinizing the files Loren had provided, but nothing had jumped out at him. Dominique's friend Misha Saunders's details proved entirely correct. The one thing she did not mention was Dominique's mother's name. Was that the missing link to this puzzle?

Chris found the rack card he had gotten from Dominique's office, which mentioned that she had received her law degree from Columbia Law School in New York, one of the country's best ranked and most expensive schools. The question remained: How had she afforded the tuition? The acceptance rate to the school was extremely low.

Bingo!

Yolanda Lucia Juárez—Dominique's mother. Chris noticed that she did not have the same last name as Dominique. Was this because she was not married to Dominique's father, or was she not Dominique and Darcy's mother?

Chris was tempted to reschedule his date with Lydia and call Dominique back. Though he did not consider this a date in the romantic sense. More like spending time with a good friend, as he and Lydia had much in common.

In the end he opted not to call. He did not want to seem overzealous, and he wanted to do some more digging—plus it wouldn't hurt to make Dominique sweat a little.

Lydia had tickets to see John Legend at the Schermerhorn Symphony Center in Nashville. Chris had seen his incredible performance a few years ago in Vegas. The concert was scheduled to start at 7:30 p.m., and considering the thirty-minute drive from Brentwood to the venue, Chris had taken proactive measures by securing hotel reservations for an overnight stay.

Chris arrived at Lydia's house at four with the car fueled and bags packed. This would give them plenty of time to reach the hotel, shower, and get dressed for the concert. The ride to Nashville was relaxing. Every moment spent with Lydia unveiled a new layer of her personality. This time was no different. He discovered that she adored her extended family, cherished her close bond with her parents, and treasured being the only child.

The concert was fantastic. John lived up to his name, performing all the classic hits such as "All of Me," "Glory," "Green Light," "Ordinary People," and "Tonight (Best You Ever Had)." They definitely got their money's worth. Just as the concert was about to end, Lydia leaned over and handed Chris a lanyard that read: BACKSTAGE PASS.

You would have thought Chris had won the lottery. The smile on his face was priceless. Lydia and Chris spent about fifteen minutes talking with John and received an autographed T-shirt and photo with him.

The venue was still crowded as concert attendees headed to their cars after the meet and greet. Chris and Lydia decided to get something to eat at a burger spot not far from the hotel. The burger reminded Chris of what his mother called a "back door mama" burger. The thick, juicy patty was perfectly seasoned and topped with cheese and diced onions all nested within a bun toasted to perfection. Its warmth caused the cheese to melt and the condiments to slowly ooze off the side. When Chris took a bite, he could distinctly taste the savory sour-cream-and-onion potato chips placed impeccably on the patty. He washed it down with a refreshing glass of strawberry Fanta.

Chris was so impressed with his burger that he requested to speak with the manager on duty to express how much he enjoyed his meal. The waiter escorted the manager to their table. With a bright smile and a firm hand, he introduced himself as Fritz, the owner and operator.

Fritz said the restaurant had been in his family for twenty-five years, and the burger recipe was his mother's. Fritz explained that his house had been the hangout spot as a child, and his mom had always cooked after his football and wrestling matches. So after he and his siblings had left home, his mother opened the restaurant to honor all the young men and women she had fed over the years.

Chris noticed the pride in Fritz's eyes as he talked about his mother. He mentioned that his mother still visited the restaurant at least twice a week to help in the kitchen and serve customers during busy times, especially on weekends.

Fritz's father was not mentioned, only his siblings. Chris assumed that Fritz had been raised in a single-parent home like him. This was probably why he had a fond appreciation for his mother. It has been said that boys are attached to their moms and consider them to be their first love.

After finishing their meal, Chris and Lydia returned to the hotel. Walking to their respective rooms, they chatted about the concert and their interaction with Fritz. As always, they embraced and said goodbye as they parted ways. But this embrace was different. It felt more relaxed than the other ones Chris had exchanged with Lydia. It was as if she did not want to let go, but Chris did not want to read too much into it.

When Chris entered his room, he noticed his phone flashing red, indicating he had a message. He was surprised because only Lydia and Joy knew he had taken a trip to Nashville. He had just left Lydia, and Joy had his cell phone number to reach him. Chris checked his cell phone to ensure he had not missed any calls, then called the front desk. The phone rang several times before the receptionist answered.

"Good morning. Winston Inn and Suites, this is Naomi. How can I help you?"

"Good morning, Naomi. This is Mr. Calloway in room 814. Do you have a message for me?"

"Indeed, Mr. Calloway, I wanted to inform you that we sent this message to express our gratitude for your recent stay and extend an offer for an extra day at no cost to celebrate the hotel's fiftieth anniversary."

Chris felt relieved. He had feared the worst, especially since receiving the anonymous letter. He thanked Naomi and asked if he could use the complimentary night in the future.

She said that he had a year from today to redeem the offer.

Chris had enjoyed his time in Nashville and would certainly visit again soon—if only to get a burger from Fritz's restaurant.

Chapter 12

OPEN DOOR

Anya had just finished a phone call with Leah, discussing properties and how the pregnancy was going, when her phone buzzed with a text from Terri. It was another listing, the third Terri had sent in the last thirty minutes. Anya could not help but feel her hopes dwindling for the property she had her heart set on—the one in the Arts District she had made an offer on.

Anya left to meet Terri for a property viewing just around the corner from the Airbnb. When she saw the building, it failed to meet her expectations. The architectural details were disappointingly bland, lacking the character and charm she was looking for. Just as Anya was about to turn around, Terri exited her vehicle and approached her.

"Before jumping to conclusions based on outside appearances, let's explore what's inside," Terri suggested.

"Okay," Anya agreed hesitantly. She followed Terri into the building, and the musty smell that greeted them at once raised a red flag. As they ascended the staircase, Anya's eyes widened in amazement as she stepped into an open space offering a stunning view of the Atlantic Ocean. Each area they explored revealed more breathtaking ocean views. Terri waited to show Anya the best part of the building: the rooftop terrace, which had clear views stretching as far as South Beach.

Though Anya was not entirely convinced about this property, she was still intrigued and would consider it a contender if her number one choice in the Arts District went to another buyer. After viewing two more properties, which were deemed not suitable, Terri and Anya decided to go shopping and have an early dinner.

Terri offered to drive Anya back to her suite afterward, but Anya declined, saying, "I need to walk off the five thousand calories I consumed after eating a burrito and two soft tacos with refried beans and rice."

Both ladies laughed as they bid good night to each other.

Anya felt a sense of pride as she took the short walk back to the Airbnb. Normally, she would have called Royce for his advice. But more importantly, he should have been right here with her. Anya felt utterly lost and unsure of the future for her and Royce. She started to ponder the root of her uncertainty.

What was it? Royce was the ideal partner. He provided love, respect, and security. But was that enough for Anya? Did she want something that she could not have? Or was she just being unreasonable and stubborn?

Anya made it back to the Airbnb. She entered the lobby, and on her way to the elevator she overheard a familiar voice—one she had not heard in a long time but knew very well. What were the odds of her being in the same city and staying at the same place as her ex-boyfriend? She had not heard from or seen Grayson since their breakup. A small part of her wanted to bump into him casually and show him that she was living her best life. But really, who was she trying to convince? Her life was in shambles.

Anya picked up her pace and got in the elevator. Just as the doors were nearly shut, she heard Grayson say, "Can you hold the door?"

Anya muttered to herself, "I do *not* have the energy to deal with this right now," and let the doors close. She let out a sigh as the elevator ascended to the penthouse.

Anya endured a night of restlessness. She tossed and turned as her mind was plagued by relentless thoughts. Around four in the morning, she resorted to taking a sleeping pill. But the elusive embrace of slumber remained out of reach despite her efforts. After what seemed like an eternity, Anya finally closed her eyes and began drifting off but was suddenly awakened by her phone ringing.

Anya ignored the unfamiliar number and let it go to voicemail. She expected the caller to leave a message, but they did not, nor did they call back. Eventually, the sleeping pill took effect, and she fell into a deep sleep. When she woke, it was past three in the afternoon. She felt refreshed and hungry, her stomach rumbling.

Easing herself to the edge of the bed, Anya stretched and slowly stood up.

She then walked into the bathroom and glanced at herself in the mirror before disrobing and showering.

The mist rising from the steaming water enveloped Anya, causing her locks to coil and twist at the nape of her neck. Anya felt a tingling sensation form between her legs. The hot water caressed the spot that Royce had maintained. Oh, how she missed his touch. The thought of their forever after was washing away, like the water down the drain. Anya knew too much time had passed to salvage their relationship. She quickly bathed, dried off, and dressed, then headed to the kitchen to prepare herself something to eat.

Anya craved something fiery and bold. Before coming to Miami, she had begun watching culinary shows on the Food Network. One particular recipe stuck in her mind: a Thai-inspired crispy Mongolian beef dish paired with fluffy brown rice that took less than two hours to prepare.

The fragrant aromas of ginger and garlic wafted through the air, enticing her senses and making her mouth water in anticipation. She carried her plate to the couch and turned on the television in search of a good movie. The explosion of flavors danced on her palate with each savory bite, fulfilling her spicy craving in the best way possible.

After eating, she treated herself to some homemade bread pudding from the hotel restaurant and then took a walk on the beach. As Anya laced her shoes, a soft but familiar voice called out her name, breaking the silence. Pausing momentarily, she felt a flutter of curiosity mixed with uncertainty. The voice lingered in the air, but she could not quite place it—it seemed out of context, as if it belonged to a dream rather than her reality. She glanced around, searching for the source, her heart quickening with anticipation.

Chapter 13

STILL WATERS

Sebastián awakened, drenched in sweat. This was not the first time this had happened; he had been waking up in a similar state for the past week, each night more restless than the last. As he lay there, his heart raced, and memories of his nighttime vision flooded his mind in vivid detail, replaying like a haunting film loop. He could still hear the muffled sounds and see the faces that had haunted him—each moment etched into his memory with unsettling clarity. He was convinced that this dream held the answer to who the mole was.

The doorbell rang, its sharp sound slicing through the stillness of the room and pulling Sebastián away from his wandering thoughts. He blinked a few times, momentarily disoriented as the images from his mind faded. With a deep sigh, he pushed aside the heavy bed covering, reluctant to give up its warmth and comfort. The room's cool air was a harsh shock against his damp skin. Grumbling some not-so-nice words under his breath, Sebastián swung his legs over the side of the bed and planted his feet on the chilly wooden floor. As he padded toward the door, he could hear faint voices from outside but could not make out who was waiting on the other side of the threshold.

Sebastián opened the door, eyes widening in shock. Ma and Pa Franklin, Mrs. Margaret, Ocean, and Marisa stood before him.

"Boy, you ain't nothin' but skin and bones," Ma Franklin said as she hugged him tightly with tears in her eyes. Everyone greeted Sebastián with warm embraces as they entered the house. Confused and unable to gather his thoughts, he perceived what he believed was a mirage, much like his recurring dream. Yet he did not want to wake up from this dream. In his mind, Sebastián's dream would be complete if Anya were in it.

"Daddy, how are you feeling?" Ocean asked, breaking Sebastián's train of thought.

"Baby girl, I am doing fabulous now that you all are here." He looked up with a grin. "But how on earth did you manage to persuade Ma to board a plane? I've been trying to get her out of Tennessee for years!"

"That's a good question," Pa said. "All I know is that Ma said she talked to a French agent. Can't remember her name though." Sebastián knew precisely who that French woman was.

Sebastián had not spent much time with Alex since their dinner at the Mediterranean café. It was as if she was avoiding him. He had called her multiple times, but his calls had gone unanswered. Sebastián could only surmise that the events on the boat had taken a toll on her.

"Where is the kitchen?" Ma and Mrs. Margaret asked in perfect harmony.

Their voices echoed through the room, triggering a wave of laughter. The cheerful sound bounced off the walls as Sebastián playfully gestured toward the kitchen, a mischievous grin spreading across his face.

Sebastián's stomach began to rumble as the sinful aroma from the kitchen started to fill the room. He could smell a mixture of bacon, blueberry pancakes, and coffee. These were the sounds and smells of home. Something that Sebastián had missed. Tears began to fill his eyes as he remembered his conversation with Mr. Baxter. Was he willing to give up this to advance in his career?

"Hey, son, can we go for a walk?" Pa said. Sebastián knew what that meant. He nodded and walked Pa outside onto the back deck, a quaint space that exuded a sense of warmth and comfort. The same comfort he had felt as a young child underneath the giant oak tree not far from the apartment back home. The sweet scent of the blooms mingled with the fresh, earthy aroma of the surrounding garden, creating an atmosphere that felt like a peaceful retreat from the world. It was an ideal setting for meaningful conversations or simply soaking in the moment's serenity together.

"So, what got you so riled up?" Pa asked.

Sebastián took a moment to contemplate whether he should tell him about his conversation with Mr. Baxter. "Nothing, Pa. I just wasn't expecting to see you all—especially you and Ma. This ordeal has made me rethink my life and the direction in which it is going. The thought of not being here to see you all and

Ocean has made me reconsider many things."

Pa sat quietly for a few minutes.

"Does that include your relationships and career?" he asked. "Yes," Sebastián replied.

"Life lessons are the building blocks that create the person we become. If you allow yourself to be weighed down by fear, you'll never experience life's unexpected joys. Remember, you never want to reach my age and say, 'could've, would've, should've.' Clarifying moments of uncertainty uncovers opportunities for prosperity and growth. You possess the strength and resilience to navigate life's twists and turns. Remember, you're a Franklin."

With a firm pat on Sebastián's shoulder, Pa turned and headed back inside. Sebastián stood there momentarily, pondering how his grandfather always knew exactly what to say to guide him through his moments of doubt and indecision. It was as if Pa had an uncanny ability to pull him back from the edge of uncertainty and redirect his focus toward the possibilities that lay ahead.

Sebastián knew that his decision would affect his life personally and professionally. But for now, he wanted to spend time with his family while they were here.

Thanks to Ocean, Ma, and Mrs. Margaret, breakfast was delicious. Later that evening, Sebastián took the family on a city tour. As they strolled through the bustling streets, Sebastián shared stories about the historical landmarks and hidden gems, allowing them to soak in the city's vibrant atmosphere while marveling at its architecture and culture.

Sebastián could not take credit for knowing all the city had to offer. He had learned much of it from Alex when they had taken in the sights together. When Mrs. Margaret asked about Alex and Mr. Baxter, Sebastián quickly said they were both on an assignment.

"Is that the French lady I spoke with?" Ma asked. "Yes," Sebastián said.

"So who is Mr. Baxter?"

"He's the agent in charge of the field office I'm assigned here in Lyon." "Well I hope to meet Mr. Baxter and thank him for taking good care of you," Ma said with a pointed look. Mrs. Margaret nodded in agreement.

"He's a great guy, and you both would like him," he replied, smiling softly.

* * *

Sebastián thoroughly enjoyed the week he spent with his family, creating lasting memories before their imminent return to the States. Despite the joy of their time together, he could not shake a persistent unease, mainly because he had not heard from Alex or Mr. Baxter. While he felt little concern about Mr. Baxter's silence— given his role within the agency—Alex's lack of communication struck him as odd. She was usually reliable, going with him to appointments or checking to see how he was doing.

Motivated by curiosity and concern, he called the agency's office to check on Alex's whereabouts. After a brief conversation, he discovered that she was not currently on assignment, which only deepened his confusion. Reluctant to wait any longer, he decided to visit her apartment since she was not responding to his calls.

Sebastián arrived at Alex's flat thirty minutes later. He scanned the street for any sign of her motorcycle. Relief washed over him as he spotted the sleek black bike parked neatly next to a row of shrubs. The familiar sight of her beloved ride brought a smile to his face as he stepped out of the car, feeling a mix of anticipation and nervousness as he approached the entrance to her building.

Just as he crossed the street, the door to the building opened, and to his surprise, Alex walked out. And she was not alone.

Chapter 14

MISUNDERSTOOD

The start of the work week was unlike any other. On Sunday evening, while driving back from Nashville, Chris received a text message from Dominique saying they needed to reschedule their meeting to next week. There was no explanation— not that she had to, but Chris thought it would have been nice.

On Tuesday, Lydia called and informed him that she had tested positive for COVID-19, which they both assumed she had contracted at the concert. Chris took the necessary precautions, left work, and immediately got tested. As he suspected, he was also positive. He called Joy, informed her of his status, and asked that the staff be tested.

Chris took the recommended five days off work and stayed isolated, remaining symptom-free, including without a fever for twenty-four hours. After that, he wore a mask around others for five more days to reduce the chance of spreading the virus. He felt fortunate that he had not suffered any virus-related symptoms. The same could not be said for Lydia. She experienced severe fatigue, loss of taste and smell, and muscle and body aches. He called to check on her daily and brought her meals while she was in isolation.

Chris contacted Dominique and rescheduled their meeting after ten days had passed. They met at the Sunset Soul Bistro for a late dinner. When Chris entered the restaurant, Dominique was already seated and reviewing the menu.

He slowly approached the table and said, "Everything on the menu is good, but I recommend the smothered chicken, macaroni and cheese, cabbage, cornbread, and a side of jerk oxtails."

Startled by his voice, Dominique accidentally spilled her water on the table, which cascaded onto the floor. Chris quickly grabbed the napkins from the table and began wiping up the spill. Before long, the server came and proceeded to mop the floor and move them to a nearby table.

Dominique's cheeks flushed with embarrassment as she realized the scene she had caused. She whispered an apology for her clumsiness before excusing herself from the table and going to the restroom. Meanwhile, Chris sat there, feeling utterly foolish about the mishap, his mind racing about how to lighten the mood after such an unexpected turn of events.

Chris stood up as Dominique approached the table. He pulled the chair out for her to sit in. "I sincerely apologize for startling you," Chris said, his voice filled with concern. "If you prefer to leave, I completely understand."

Dominique's response was steady, her tone calm yet measured. "There's no need for that; I'm perfectly fine. Let's focus on the matter at hand."

The air between them grew dense and icy, reminiscent of the frigid winds of Antarctica. Chris felt he had demonstrated a noble gesture by offering an exit, but the weight of the silence around them only deepened his apprehension.

He responded with the same calmness. "What did you want to discuss, Ms.

Sanchez, regarding your client, Mr. White? I hope you have the semen analysis report we requested."

Dominque reached into her leather bag and handed Chris a file. As he read the report, Chris began to laugh. "Is this a joke?" After weeks of waiting, the results were inconclusive, and the report did not explain why.

"Ms. Sanchez, as I've told you before, don't let this coy smile and relaxed demeanor fool you. I ask you with the utmost respect—please do not take me for a fool. I suggest you speak with your client and make it clear to him that if I do not get a report by the close of business next Friday, I'll be forced to call in a few favors, which will include going to Mr. White's place of employment to have the sample collected."

Chris slowly stood, reached into his pocket, placed one hundred dollars on the table, and bid Dominique good night.

He felt his temper rising as he walked to his car. The one thing he had inherited from his father was a temper, which he worked hard to control. Opening the door to his vehicle, he sat collecting his thoughts as he contemplated his next move. He knew he would not mention this meeting to Royce until he received the conclusive evidence. Chris saw firsthand the toll this was having on him.

Dominique finally emerged from the restaurant with a bag in hand. He watched as she walked to her car and drove out of the parking lot, closely followed by two black Chevy Suburbans with tinted windows and diplomat flags on the hoods.

Chris thought that was strange. Why would two SUVs simultaneously pull out of the parking lot shortly after Dominique? Fortunately, Chris had a photogenic memory, so he jotted down the license plate numbers on the file Dominique had given him.

Something did not add up! Did Dominique know she was being followed? "Siri, dial Montana," Chris instructed.

A voice came through after several rings. "You better have a good reason for calling me during Thursday night football." The sounds of lively conversation and laughter floated through the line, blending with the distant cheers and the muffled crackle of the TV playing in the background.

Chris chuckled. "I do," he assured him. Montana was Chris's frat brother and a jack of all trades. He reminded Chris of Tommy from the nineties sitcom *Martin*. Whenever Chris asked about his job, he never gave a straight answer.

"Montana, I need you to investigate Nate White's and Dominique Sanchez's backgrounds." Chris provided the necessary context for his inquiry and gave Montana the license plate numbers of the suspicious vehicles he had seen in the parking lot.

"How soon do you need the information?" Montana asked. "By tomorrow."

"Wow! Okay, I will see what I can do," replied Montana.

The drive home was a whirlwind of thoughts and emotions for Chris, the weight of uncertainty pressing heavily on his mind. As he navigated the familiar roads, he could not shake off the nagging questions that plagued him. What if his gut feeling about Dominique was wrong? Each turn of the wheel echoed his worries, amplifying the doubts that danced in his head. He replayed their conversations, searching for clues that might affirm or dispel his suspicions.

Chapter 15

A PLAN OF ACTION

Royce recently received uplifting news from Doctor Willis after undergoing a stress echocardiogram. The results showed that his heart was functioning perfectly, with no abnormalities detected. This positive outcome relieved and motivated him to prioritize his health even more.

Embracing this fresh start, with the help of a dietician, Royce began significantly transforming his eating habits. He now opted for nutrient-dense foods like leafy greens, berries, and citrus fruits and reduced his soda intake. He also introduced lean proteins, such as grilled chicken and fish, and wholesome grains, like quinoa and brown rice, ensuring each meal is balanced and satisfying.

Royce had just finished an intense workout at the gym when his phone rang as he walked toward his car. It was Bryce.

"Hey, bro," Royce answered, wiping his brow with the back of his hand. "What's up? Do you have time to chat?"

"Yeah, I do," Bryce replied, his tone unusually serious. Royce instantly sensed that something was weighing on his mind. He sat in the driver's seat, preparing for whatever news Bryce had to share.

"Bro, I've been feeling really frustrated lately. Leah's mood swings make it hard to know what to expect. She's all over the place. As a result, I've slept on the couch for the past two nights, trying to find some peace and space away from the chaos. And now I'm headed to the airport to catch a flight to Tennessee."

Royce realized he had not told Bryce about his situation with Anya, and, by all accounts, neither had Leah. He knew he would eventually have to, but now was not a good time.

Bryce's flight was due to arrive at 7:20 p.m. He was flying in from Mississippi after meeting Leah's extended family and celebrating her father's birthday. Bryce still lived in Florida, but since he and Leah were expecting, he had been dividing his time between Florida and Tennessee.

Royce found it odd that Leah had not mentioned that he and Anya were no longer together. His emotional bond with Anya seemed to have slipped through the cracks. However, in his heart, the reality was different. He clung to the idea that he and Anya were still together, navigating their separation with hope and longing. The thought of his relationship with Anya drifting into the past weighed heavily on him, leaving him caught in a limbo between acceptance and denial.

Bryce's flight was twenty minutes late due to a thunderstorm coming off the coast of Florida. Memories of his time with Anya in Florida made Royce miss her and reminded him how uncomfortable she was with storms.

Royce glanced at the weather forecast on his cell phone, and to his dismay, the radar report revealed a severe storm brewing in Jacksonville. Dark clouds loomed ominously on the horizon, indicating that heavy rainfall was expected to drench the Miami area for the next two days.

Royce quickly texted Bryce his location and dialed Anya's number. The phone rang multiple times before going to voicemail. Royce was not surprised. It had been two months since they had spoken and seen one another. He attempted to call again, but she still did not answer, so he sent a text message. *Hi Anya. I'm not expecting you to respond. I know it's been a while since we spoke, but I wanted to check on you. Please be safe. A severe thunderstorm is approaching. I love you.*

A series of animated bubbles appeared in the text field, indicating Anya was typing. They appeared and disappeared several times before finally disappearing altogether.

Royce knew to leave well enough alone and said a silent prayer as a call came in from Bryce.

"Hey Royce, I'm standing in front of door four."

Royce spotted him immediately as he pulled up to the curb just in front of the taxicab pulling out.

Bryce quickly placed his luggage in the vehicle's rear and got in. Royce noticed that Bryce had grown out his beard, which was well-manicured, highlighting the salt-and-pepper look.

"Hi, bro," Bryce said as he closed the car door. "It's good to see you." Before Royce could respond, Bryce began discussing what was happening with Leah and her unpredictable mood swings.

Royce listened attentively to his brother, who clearly needed to vent his frustration. "Well, Bryce, you know she's pregnant with *your* baby. And we know how difficult you can be . . ." Royce grinned as Bryce gave him a playful shove.

It was as if a lightbulb had gone off in Bryce's brain.

"By the way," Royce said, "what's with this new look? I like it. You look very distinguished."

Bryce smiled, rubbing his hand along his jawline.

Royce continued, "Leah is carrying a human being, and her hormones are everywhere. You know you should've called Mom. She's the best person to ask; she's had three crumb snatchers."

Bryce grew silent, suddenly realizing that this might be a sensitive subject for Royce. He had lost not only Skylar but also a baby he would never know.

"I'm being a real jerk," Bryce said. "Here I am, rambling on and not thinking about you."

"It's okay, man. I know this is new for you and Leah, so I understand," Royce said. "When will Leah be returning from Mississippi?"

"She'll be back on Monday." Bryce paused. "Where's Anya?" he asked. "She's in Miami checking on properties for the satellite office."

Bryce gave Royce a curious glance. "Why aren't you there with her?"

Royce let out a gusty sigh. He could not lie to Bryce. So he shared the details of his situation involving Anya and Bria.

"Man, I thought my life was full of drama!" Bryce shook his head. "We both need a drink or two. I'll buy us a few rounds," he said, patting Royce on the shoulder. The brothers laughed as they headed to the nearest bar.

* * *

The night before was a complete fog. Royce groaned softly as he became aware of his surroundings, an insistent pulse pounding in his temples, promising a lingering hangover. He cracked one eye open, squinting against the muffled light that filtered through the heavy curtains. It took him a moment to process his location: his couch, its fabric rough against his skin, and the unpleasant odor of liquor hanging heavily in the air around him. The disarray of empty bottles and half-eaten snacks littering the coffee table was a testament to the previous night's debauchery—a reminder of his guy's night out with Bryce.

Royce called Bryce's name to ensure he was in the house. Massaging his temples, Royce slowly eased up from the couch and walked toward the guest bedroom, but it was empty. Entering the bathroom, he found Bryce sleeping in the bathtub—an amusing sight. He thought it best to let him sleep off the liquor that he had consumed.

Royce retreated to his bedroom and climbed into bed, allowing his eyelids to droop heavily. Soon, he surrendered to the pull of sleep, the image of Bryce in the bathtub fading from his mind as the warmth of slumber enveloped him.

When Royce entered the kitchen later, Bryce handed him a bottle of Gatorade, a sandwich, and some Aleve. As he sat at the table, Royce could still feel the effects of his hangover.

"So when was the last time you spoke with Anya?" Bryce asked. Royce rubbed his face. "Been a while."

"Can you be more specific? "Almost two months."

"And she hasn't called you either?"

"No." Royce took a bite of his sandwich. "I'm surprised Leah didn't mention it to you."

"Aw, you know women are known to keep secrets," Bryce replied. "But to be honest, I don't think Anya has told her. I know that Leah spoke with her a few days ago . . ."

"Bryce, be honest with me. Do you think I'm wrong for wanting to know the truth?"

"Absolutely not! Would I have communicated things differently? Yes, probably. I would've told Anya about the phone call with Bria and the retaking of the paternity test. Anya's actions tell me she fears losing you and the changes that would happen if Mia is yours."

Royce nodded. "I hear you. But I have reassured Anya that nothing will change if Mia is my daughter."

"Yes, you may have. But remember, Bria is also a part of this equation, and Anya is still working through her past traumas and trust issues."

"How many more times can I tell her I'm here till the end? I have expressed this through my words and actions."

"That answer depends on you and Anya. Or perhaps you should consider calling it quits. I realize love doesn't require us to be perfect but to listen, and I am learning that concept each day."

Bryce's words were reassuring and helped clarify his relationship with Anya. In the words of Mr. Overton, *Whatever you are going through, this too shall pass. Trust in the process; your time to love again is coming.*

"A drunk mind speaks the sober truth," he said to Bryce.

Chapter 16

CAUTIOUS

Sebastián watched as the door to Alex's flat opened. Alex stepped out first, followed by Chief Inspector Wellington and Riff. Alex's confident stride and warm smile seemed dim as she casually slid into the sedan's back seat, which had pulled up to the curb. Her movements were fluid yet deliberate.

Wellington took the front passenger seat, his eyes scanning the surroundings with a watchful intensity. Riff, eager as ever, joined Alex in the back, settling beside her with a loyal glance. Sebastián squinted through the tinted windows, catching a glimpse of a shadowy figure nestled in the corner of the back seat. The presence of this figure created a sense of mystery in the already tense atmosphere. The vehicle's door shut quietly as it sped off down the street.

Something felt off. Throughout his time with Alex, Sebastián had noticed that whenever she was in the same room as Chief Inspector Wellington, she always made a point to sit far away from him. There was no direct contact or interaction, so seeing her get into a vehicle with him and Riff was unusual.

Sebastián did not know whether to follow the vehicle or contact Mr. Baxter, who had told him that there was a mole in the office. Should he call Tess or Lugo? He went with his gut feeling.

"Hi, Captain Reynolds. Can you please run some names for me?" Sebastián had been in close contact with Captain Reynolds since his release from the hospital. Sebastián had not told him about his conversation with Mr. Baxter because he had not yet decided. Captain Reynolds took down the information and told Sebastián he would get back to him within twenty-four hours.

Sebastián replayed his conversation with Alex and Mr. Baxter in his head.

Was there a connection? What was he missing? After waiting in front of Alex's flat for another thirty minutes, hoping they would return, Sebastián decided to leave.

Just as he placed the car in drive, his phone vibrated, indicating a text message had come in. He opened the message, noticing it was from an unknown number. *Go to the garden behind the flat and retrieve the instructions from underneath the flowerpot closest to the door on the right.*

Placing his hand on his service weapon, Sebastián scanned the area for any suspicious vehicles or people. His senses were heightened. He knew someone must be watching him from afar. Taking precautions, Sebastián crouched in the driver's seat, turned the ignition, and put the car in drive. Easing off the brake, the vehicle rolled forward as he maneuvered out of the tight parking space. Reaching the end of the block, Sebastián peered into the rearview mirror, and there, in the middle of the street, stood a man whose posture was rigid, his gaze fixed directly on Sebastián.

A chill ran down his spine. The man seemed out of place, as if he were waiting for something—or someone. Reacting quickly, Sebastián made a sharp right turn onto an adjacent street. His instincts kicked in as he focused on the road, yet just as he turned, a pedestrian unexpectedly stepped off the curb into the car's path. In that split second, Sebastián barely swerved in time to avoid a collision, adrenaline coursing through his veins as he gripped the steering wheel tightly, determined to maintain control.

After quickly bringing the car to a complete stop, Sebastián exited the vehicle to ensure the pedestrian was not injured. To his relief, the gentleman was fine, just a bit shaken up.

Sebastián had a feeling that the man he had seen in his rearview mirror was there for either him, Alex, or both. He hesitated to return home because he had no idea if he was still being followed. Therefore, he chose to stay at a hotel outside Lyon.

Sebastián did not sleep at all. He tossed and turned, and the little sleep he did manage to get was interrupted by dreams of the previous day's events and the hostage situation on the boat. Strangely, his conversation with Alex and Mr. Baxter had also entered his dreams. He followed his therapist's advice and started detailing every aspect of the dream, including the conversations, in writing.

The one thing that stuck out in Sebastian's mind was Alex's statement: *I saw the red beam of light aimed at me. I've replayed that scene in my head every day since it happened.*

Was Alex also aware that there was a mole in the agency? Maybe this was why she had gotten into the vehicle with Wellington and Riff. Had they kidnapped her?

He decided to call Mr. Baxter. "Good morning, sir. I'm sorry to bother you so early. I won't take up too much of your time, but are you available to meet with me to discuss our last conversation?"

"Of course," Mr. Baxter replied. "I always have time for you, Sebastián.

I'm heading to the field office, so we can meet there."

Sebastián hesitated, feeling a twinge of apprehension. "Mr. Baxter, would it be possible to meet somewhere else?" he asked, trying to gauge the situation.

"Where do you have in mind?" Mr. Baxter inquired, sounding curious.

Sebastián took a deep breath and gave Mr. Baxter the name and address of a cozy local bookstore known for its quiet atmosphere and comfortable seating. Despite the serious nature of the meeting, Sebastián could not shake his unease about Mr. Baxter's true intentions. To be safe, he arrived at the bookstore an hour early to survey the surroundings and ensure everything felt secure.

As he approached the bookstore, Sebastián's heart raced. He carefully scanned the area for any signs of trouble. Satisfied that everything appeared normal, he found a discreet spot near the entrance to keep watch. After a few minutes, he spotted Mr. Baxter stepping out of his vehicle, adjusting his coat as he walked toward the bookstore's entrance.

Once Mr. Baxter entered, Sebastián waited a moment longer before following him inside. The warm, inviting smell of old books surrounded him, calming his nerves slightly. He cautiously made his way through the aisles until he spotted Mr. Baxter. He was seated in a comfortable armchair near the history section, deeply engrossed in a book titled *Frederick Douglass: From Slave to Statesman*. Mr. Baxter's concentration on the book seemed genuine, yet Sebastián remained alert, unsure of what this meeting would ultimately reveal.

Sebastián approached, pulling Mr. Baxter from the pages of his book. He stood up as they greeted each other with a firm handshake and a sincere good morning.

When they had settled into the chairs, Mr. Baxter smiled and began to speak. "What a charming bookstore this is! I've heard so much about it and have been eager to stop by for quite some time," he remarked, his eyes scanning the shelves bursting with colorful titles. Then, turning his attention to Sebastián, he asked, "Are you an avid reader?"

"I dabble here and there," Sebastián said. "I see you are a fan of the art of literacy."

Mr. Baxter nodded. "I've always found that immersing yourself in reading allows you to envision the world beyond your own door."

He then opened the book and leaned toward Sebastián, turning the page to reveal a slip of paper with a handwritten note that read: *Two men who walked in after you are sitting 100 meters from us. I noticed them in the parking lot just as I came in.*

Mr. Baxter engaged Sebastián in conversation, keeping an air of casualness as if everything were perfectly normal. However, Sebastián felt a growing sense of unease and discreetly started to assess his surroundings. His eyes darted around the room, searching for the nearest exits in case he needed to make a swift escape. In his quick survey, he identified four clearly marked exit routes, each offering a potential path to safety. He focused intently on the men nearby, trying to gauge any changes in their demeanor that might signal trouble.

Sebastián's phone pinged, indicating he had a message. He did not want to retrieve the text from his phone, so he glanced at his smartwatch to read the message. It was from Captain Reynolds. *Please confirm Mr. Baxter's first name.*

Sebastián quickly typed in the information requested. Seconds later, Captain Reynolds advised that the name did not appear in their database. However, another name did.

Chapter 17

DÉJÀ VU

Anya lifted her gaze, shielding her eyes from the sun's rays as she anticipated the source of the mysterious voice.

"It's been a long time," said a deep masculine voice.

Anya recognized it immediately when she heard his hearty laugh. "Grayson," she replied, "it has indeed been a very long time." "When I checked in yesterday, I thought that was you in the lobby."

"Oh?" Anya said, feigning ignorance. She inquired about where he was staying, and as expected, his answer was the Historical Art Deco Penthouse and Suites.

Grayson gave her an appreciative gaze and said, "You look amazing."

Anya smiled graciously and thanked him for the compliment. But what she really wanted to say was, *Ending things with you was the best decision I ever made.*

"So what brings you to Miami?" Grayson asked.

"Business," Anya replied.

"Are you still in Tennessee, or has the company expanded to other locations?"

Anya responded affirmatively to both questions, her confidence radiating in her voice.

"That's truly impressive," Grayson remarked, a smile spreading across his face. "I never doubted for a second that you would be successful."

Yet as his words hung in the air, an unexpected shift took place. Anya's mind flashed back to being crouched in a dim, claustrophobic elevator, her heart racing. A chilling wave of silence enveloping her rendered her voiceless and consumed by fear.

Not wanting to allow herself to be the victim any longer, and longing to end this nightmare, Anya blurted out, "If you had no doubt, then *why* did you abandon me and make me feel as if the assault was my fault? For *years*, I believed I was damaged goods and unworthy of love. I carried the shame from that night and the aftermath of a pregnancy that resulted from it. I could not bear the possibility of wondering whether the baby was yours or my assailant's. So I chose to terminate the pregnancy. I chose to be free and *live*, not merely just exist."

Anya shuddered from the release of her pent-up feelings. She knew this was her breakthrough, and it felt good.

Grayson stood in silence, absorbing the words Anya had just spoken. He grappled with the reality that he had abandoned her and a baby he knew nothing about. Had he really been that cold back then? The answer quickly erupted in his mind: *Yes*.

Grayson knew he had no right to question her decision to terminate the pregnancy. At the time he had not been in a position to care—mentally or financially—for Anya and a baby.

With a look of remorse, he told her, "I never intended to take you or our relationship for granted. I'm a different man now, and my priorities have changed drastically. I realized I was immature and lacked the skills to be a partner. Back then I was stuck in my past hurts and traumas, and I was operating in survival mode. And I'm genuinely sorry. I hope you have found happiness with someone who deserves you because you are unique, and he is a lucky man. Can you please forgive me and start over as friends?"

Anya could see the genuine emotion reflected in Grayson's eyes and the earnestness etched on his face. Each word he spoke carried a weight that resonated deeply with her, revealing a sincerity that made her heart soften.

Grayson and Anya stayed on the beach, reminiscing about old times and sharing current life events. As they talked, Grayson mentioned that he was in Miami with his girlfriend, excitedly preparing to embark on a cruise to the idyllic islands of the Western Caribbean. The atmosphere shifted as dark clouds gathered overhead, casting shadows over the sandy beach. Suddenly, the sky opened up, and large raindrops began to fall, quickly transforming into a steady downpour that caused them to seek refuge under a nearby palm tree.

They waited, hoping for a break in the rain. Instead, the storm grew fiercer, with heavy drops drumming relentlessly against the ground and splashing up muddy puddles around their feet. Each moment stretched on as the sky darkened further, and the sound of the rain became a deafening roar. After twenty minutes of waiting, they decided to return to the Airbnb because the rain was unlikely to stop soon. By the time they entered the lobby, they were completely soaked.

Anya graciously thanked Grayson for their heartfelt conversation before heading upstairs to change and shower. She recognized that this was no mere chance encounter; it had been intentional and orchestrated by the Most High God. As Anya stepped into the elevator, she noticed the skies growing even darker. The boats at the pier swayed back and forth as the winds picked up. It felt as though history was repeating itself, leaving her with no one to rely on but herself.

After showering, Anya gathered the wet clothes from the floor and placed her cell phone on the sink. The emergency response alert began to go off, indicating high winds and rain were approaching, producing a category-one hurricane. Anya noticed she had missed a call and text from Royce, expressing his concern for her with the approaching storm.

She started to respond but hesitated, struggling to get her thoughts together. She replayed the conversation she had had with Grayson in her mind. *I hope you have found happiness with someone who deserves you because you are unique, and he is a lucky man.*

Anya recognized that she was incredibly fortunate. Royce was everything she had hoped for and needed in her life. When she called his number, it went straight to voicemail. She tried to call several more times but without success. She texted him but still received no response.

Determined to reach Royce, Anya dialed his office number. Her heart raced with anticipation as she waited for the call to connect. However, to her surprise, the voice on the other end informed her that Royce had taken a leave of absence. This news left her feeling puzzled and concerned, and she wondered what might have prompted him to step away from work.

Was she the reason for the leave? Had she truly been so consumed by her emotions that she had overlooked everything else? Anya felt a heavy weight of guilt settle in her chest as she reflected on her recent actions. The realization hit her like a cold wave: She had allowed her personal traumas to cloud her judgment and impact those around her. It was time for her to take responsibility and repair the rifts she had caused. She needed to confront the situation directly and find a way to make amends with Royce.

The following two days brought heavy rain, but the sun was shining again by the third day. Anya spoke with Leah to explain the situation between her and Royce. During their conversation, Leah updated Anya on what had been happening with Royce. According to Bryce, Royce had an upcoming meeting to discuss some reports to determine if Bria's husband could have children. After talking with Leah, Anya made a few more calls, one of them to Terri, and went to bed as she had a busy day ahead of her tomorrow.

Chapter 18

BLACKOUT

A sudden knock at the door jolted Chris from his concentration as he reviewed his caseload for the upcoming week. He had been poring over files and notes, mentally preparing for the challenges ahead, when the sound interrupted his thoughts. Intrigued and slightly apprehensive, Chris rose from his desk and made his way to the door. Peering through the peephole, he was taken aback to find none other than Montana standing there.

This past Friday, they had discussed Montana's meticulously gathered intelligence on Dominique and Nate White. Chris found Montana's insights intriguing and somewhat troubling, a mix that set his mind racing with possibilities and concerns. Montana's unexpected visit added an air of suspense, building Chris's anticipation even further.

During their previous conversation, Montana had disclosed some alarming details about Nate White: He had been dishonorably discharged from the military, a serious mark against his character, primarily due to his grave mishandling of top-secret files. This revelation left Chris uneasy, knowing the potential implications for national security and how such a person could influence events around them.

On the other hand, Chris knew everything about Dominique; he had already done his homework and thoroughly studied her background. As Chris opened the door to greet Montana, he couldn't shake the feeling that new and potentially significant information awaited him. What critical updates or revelations would Montana unveil today? The thought intrigued and unnerved him as Chris prepared himself for any surprises.

"Hey there, brotha! Come on in," Chris greeted with a warm smile, his voice filled with curiosity.

Montana stepped inside, offering Chris a half-embrace as he crossed the threshold into the inviting space.

"What have you gotten yourself into this time?" Montana asked, raising an eyebrow, giving Chris a scrutinizing gaze.

Chris met Montana's concerned look with a puzzled expression, his mind racing to decipher the underlying question behind his friend's words.

"Nothing that I'm aware of," Chris said.

"I know you knew Dominique has a twin sister, but what if I told you she has a twin brother?"

Montana handed Chris a birth record for a baby boy named Dominic Edwardo Mercado Sanchez. As Chris examined the document, he noticed that the father's and mother's names were blacked out. This omission confused Chris because the rack card he had obtained from Dominique's office listed her mother's name as Yolanda Lucia Juárez. Chris could not understand why the birth record did not match that information. Dominique's friend Misha Saunders claimed she was from Cuba, but the document revealed that Dominic was born in San Juan, Puerto Rico.

Chris felt overwhelmed as he tried to piece everything together. What was he missing?

"No, I didn't know Dominique had a twin brother. I wonder if she is aware of it . . ." Chris said. "Were you able to find anything on the license plates I gave you?"

"Yes and no," Montana replied. "The plates are diplomat tags registered to the Madagascar Embassy, but I couldn't determine who was driving the vehicles."

Chris placed the extra documents from Montana in his vault, along with other important paperwork, for safekeeping. As he organized the files, he felt a mixture of anxiety and anticipation about his upcoming meeting with Dominique, scheduled for the end of the week. They would discuss the results of the semen analysis, and he could not help but pray that the findings would be favorable for Royce, whose future depended on this critical information.

* * *

The week dragged on, each day blending into the next as if time was at a standstill. Chris found himself immersed in a relentless pursuit, analyzing every detail of Dominique's cases. His mind raced as he sought to uncover any tangible connection between her past work and the victims of human trafficking involving Bria and Lucas. His frustration grew with each passing hour, but his determination to uncover the truth kept him engaged in the daunting task.

With Friday just a day away, a sense of apprehension settled over Chris like a thick fog. It felt like he was about to step into the courtroom for the first time, his heart racing and his palms sweating, gripped by the fear of the unknown. Each tick of the clock heightened his anxiety, reminiscent of novice lawyers wrestling with the weight of their first case—unsure of themselves yet eager to prove their worth. He could almost hear the echo of his voice in that solemn room, filled with doubt yet also a flicker of determination. He knew this moment would define his path and the paths of Royce and Mia. It loomed over him, intensifying his nerves with every passing second.

Chris picked up the phone and dialed Royce's number, eager to share details about his upcoming meeting with Dominique. As he spoke, he outlined the agenda and the key discussion points he planned to cover. Royce interjected, saying he would attend the meeting, and Chris understood why. He then gave Royce the time and location of the meeting.

Chris then called Lydia, who mentioned that she still hadn't heard from Bria. However, she said that Bria's brother Kane had contacted her earlier in the week. Although Lydia received his message, she hadn't had the chance to speak with him yet, leaving her with unanswered questions about Bria's well-being and the reasons for her silence.

* * *

The meeting was scheduled for six o'clock Friday evening at Lydia's office. For extra precaution, Chris had Montana set up surveillance in the area. He arrived early to chat privately with Lydia and catch up because they had not seen each other since their trip to Nashville.

As he waited for her in the lobby, Royce walked in. Catching up with Lydia would have to wait. The receptionist escorted them to the conference room and mentioned that Lydia would be in shortly.

Chris had not seen Royce since he had taken a personal leave of absence from the firm. At the time, he had not looked like himself. But today was different. He no longer looked weary and wore a "taking care of business" attitude.

Lydia entered the room while Chris and Royce talked. Chris introduced them as they waited for Dominique and Nate to arrive. He began to lay out his notes and files when it occurred to him that he hadn't asked Royce if he had received the paternity test results. Just as he was about to ask, Dominique walked in, alone. Chris had expected to see Nate with her.

Chris wasted no time addressing the matter at hand. He inquired about the results of the analysis, which confirmed that Nate could conceive a child. The question now was whether he was Mia's father. Just as the results were about to be read, the receptionist interrupted the meeting, informing Lydia that a gentleman was insisting on speaking with her. Lydia excused herself, which allowed Chris to ask Royce if he had received his results.

Royce pulled a sealed envelope from his suit pocket, laying it on the table in front of him. Then he said, "I am ready to breathe and live life. I've been on this merry-go-round far too long."

Lydia returned and requested to speak with Chris and Dominique privately in her office. They returned several minutes later, Chris looking stoic as he took a seat. Lydia sat back down at the head of the table.

"There has been a change of events in this matter," Lydia said calmly. "Mr. Blackmon, we have been informed you have yet to open your results. Could you please open them?"

Royce took a deep breath and slowly opened the envelope.

The probability of paternity is 99.99%.

Royce was confused. How could that be if it had been determined that Nate was Mia's father?

"Mr. Blackmon, please read the name of the child in question." "Myles Ambrose Blackmon," he said slowly.

It still had not registered in Royce's mind. Chris, recognizing that Royce was in shock, said quietly, "Bria had twins. And you are the father of Myles."

Lydia spoke up. "Kincaid Gregory, better known to you, Mr. Blackmon, as Kane—Bria's brother—was the gentleman eager to meet with me. He left this letter and asked that it be given to you."

With slightly shaking hands, Royce reached for the letter and read it silently.

Royce,

If you're reading this letter, I'm no longer here, and Kane has honored my request. First, I must start by saying I'm sorry for the turmoil I've caused you these past months. It was never supposed to be like this. When I found out I was pregnant, I was in shock, which turned into denial. Once I felt the baby move, my denial shifted into protective mode. I knew I had to do everything possible to keep her safe. I had no idea I was carrying twins until the night I delivered. It turned out that Myles was hiding behind his sister. After I delivered the twins, I received death threats from Lucas, who I later found out was involved in the tampering of the samples at the lab, along with my now ex- husband, Nate. Nate never wanted children, but one night after a drinking binge, we had sex, and in that same week, I had unprotected sex with you and Lucas.

Once the charges were dropped, I learned that Nate was involved in this case. Nate was a high-ranking military officer who had access to confidential files containing intelligence about the illegal drugs being transported into Tennessee from Mexico. Nate needed a way to stay out of the spotlight, so Lucas convinced him to marry me. I went along with it under the pretense that this would keep his ex-wife from claiming half of his retirement, which I later found to be invalid. I knew I needed to leave the state and plan for the twins' future without me.

I envision a future where my children are supported by someone who genuinely grasps the essence of family—that person is you, Royce Blackmon. Your deep commitment to family speaks volumes, and I have every confidence that you will embrace the role of father with love and dedication for Mia and Myles. Mia is not Lucas's or Nate's child; she is your daughter.

Child in Question- Mia Renee Royalty Blackmon Percentage of Probability- 99.99%

~Bria~

Royce could hardly believe the words that danced across the page before him. The weight of the letter felt heavy in his hands, and his thoughts spiraled in a chaotic whirlwind. Was this really happening, or was he trapped in a vivid dream? He read the letter again, slowly this time, every word etched into his mind as he sought to confirm his understanding. Tears welled up in his eyes, blurring the ink as he felt the flood of emotions overwhelm him.

Turning to Chris, his voice quivered with urgency as he asked, "Where are my children?" The question hung in the air, laden with desperation. Chris held his gaze steadily, the corner of his mouth twitching into a reassuring smile. "They're safe," he replied gently, "with their maternal grandparents out of the country."

A sense of relief washed over Royce, but it was quickly followed by an aching void in his heart. Chris continued, "They've agreed to meet us in two weeks."

Royce nodded, taking in the information, still grappling with the reality of it all. The thought of his children being far away tugged at him, but knowing they were with family brought a flicker of comfort amidst the chaos.

Royce immediately asked about Kane's whereabouts, and Chris pointed out that he was waiting in the lobby. Royce stood up and left the room to express his gratitude. However, upon reaching the lobby, he found that Kane was no longer there. The receptionist informed him that Kane had already left. Royce exited the building, hoping that Kane was still in the parking lot. Pulling out his cell phone, he dialed Kane's number. The phone rang several times before going to voicemail. Royce left a message expressing his gratitude and asked that he return his call.

Royce then fell to his knees and began to sob uncontrollably.

Mr. Overton's words pressed upon him like a reassuring touch. *Whatever you are going through, this too shall pass. Trust in the process; your time to love again is coming.*

Chapter 19

UNCOVERED

Sebastián looked at the name Captain Reynolds had texted, and his heart fell to his stomach. *Landon Baxter Jr.*

Sebastián did not have time to react. The two men who had entered the bookstore were now approaching them. Mr. Baxter gestured toward the exit at the back of the store, near the restrooms. On a silent count of three, they got up and raced toward the door. Outside, a car was waiting for them. Ushering Sebastián into the back seat, Mr. Baxter hopped in beside him, and the vehicle sped off.

Sebastián gripped his service weapon as Mr. Baxter began to speak. "Sebastián, I understand your confusion, and I can clarify: My name is

Arturo Bailey. I'm a special agent with Interpol and a friend of your father." "My father is dead!" Sebastián shouted.

"Let me explain," Mr. Bailey said. "As I mentioned, we had an agent working undercover for over a year when this case came to us. At that time, your father oversaw the field office in the south of France, where most of his cases were undercover, and he and Josiah worked closely together.

"When the commander here at the Lyon office announced his retirement, your father was chosen to replace him. Many agents had heard his name but had never seen him due to his undercover status. This is when it was discovered that we had a mole within the agency. We initially thought there was only one, but there were multiple, including Angelo, Tess, and Wellington. Alex grew suspicious after she overheard Tess discussing aborting the delivery with Wellington. She brought this to my attention, and we initiated surveillance on them. The footage shows meetings with high-ranking members of the operation, including recorded conversations with Styles, the head of the drug cartel."

Sebastián interrupted Mr. Bailey to ask how he knew his father and why the name Landon Baxter Jr. had come up in the database.

"I'm sure your mother has told you that your father served in the Air Force and was involved in a tragic accident, which is accurate; however, he did not lose his life. The night before the accident, your father placed a scripture from his mother in the cockpit as a token of protection and guidance—a ritual he followed every time he flew. On the day of the accident, your father and another airman were asked to switch planes. The planes collided, causing both men to be ejected from their aircraft and suffer severe facial burns and internal injuries. The other airman—believed to be your father—succumbed to his injuries, while your father remained in a coma for over a year, mistaken for the other airman who had no listed family. When he regained consciousness, he couldn't remember who he was or his life before the accident. But he recalled that he loved to fly, that London was a special place, and the initials L.J. seemed to mean something.

"Your father navigated life, constantly striving and reinventing himself. He climbed the ranks at Interpol, becoming the first African American to lead a major law enforcement agency. A few years ago, he began reclaiming pieces of his memory, which led him to London and reconnected him with friends from his service days. He soon realized that the puzzle of his life was beginning to come together. When we received the case that mentioned your name as the special agent from the States, a flood of additional details emerged. Leo delved into the investigation, determined to uncover your identity. On the fateful night of your accident, he rushed to your side and was struck by a profound sense of recognition when he saw your mother kneeling beside you, praying. Her whispered words carried a weight of longing, a deep wish that Leo could be there to protect you."

A heavy silence ensued as Sebastián absorbed this news. "Where is he now?" he asked sharply.

Just then, the car stopped, and the rear door swung open. Ja'Nae appeared, her face etched with a mixture of apprehension and relief. Standing beside her was a man who bore no striking resemblance and held an aura that sparked curiosity.

Leo stared at Sebastián—it was like looking into a mirror before the accident. After being told Sebastián was out of the woods, he had returned to the hospital, hoping to run into Ja'Nae. He had, just as she was about to leave. His driver had pulled up beside her, and Ja'Nae had waved to alert them that she would pull out so they could take her space. When Leo exited the vehicle, he had sensed the connection between them. As she placed her luggage in the trunk, he had approached her and asked if she needed assistance. The sound of his voice had made her pause. She had looked up then, puzzled by the face that did not match the voice. Ja'Nae had attributed this confusion to her visit with Sebastián, who sounded and looked like his father. She had thanked him, declined his offer, and began walking to the driver's side door. But before she could get in, he had said, "JJ, we have lost too much time already. Our son needs us."

Now Sebastián stared intently at the man, searching for any hint of familial similarities or deep-rooted connections. Suddenly, the words of Pa Franklin flickered in his mind—*I knew you were a Franklin because you have a birthmark on your lower back.*

Sebastián leaned in closer, his voice barely a whisper as he said, "If you're truly a Franklin, there's a unique trait that sets us apart from everyone else."

Leo's eyes sparked with curiosity as he processed the implication. He took a deep breath and slipped off his jacket in a fluid motion, unbuttoned his shirt, and revealed his toned torso. With a deliberate turn, he exposed the lower part of his back, where a distinctive birthmark—a small, irregularly shaped patch of darker skin—lay hidden beneath his clothing. The mark clearly indicated his heritage, symbolizing his and Sebastián's lineage.

Still skeptical about the authenticity of Leo's identity, Sebastián began asking a series of probing personal questions, carefully selecting some that only the younger version of Leo could answer. The topics ranged from cherished childhood memories to specific events about his parents that would have been significant to him during his formative years. This seemed like a crucial test to remove any lingering doubt about whether this was indeed the same Leo.

Ja'Nae chimed in after Leo had answered all of Sebastián's questions.

Sebastián was curious as to how long she had known about Leo. Ja'Nae provided him with the details of their encounter in the hospital parking lot. Mr. Bailey also assured Sebastián of Leo's identity and said that Leo would undergo a paternity test to confirm it.

Sounds from the police radio began transmitting more frequently. Sebastián could hear Alex's voice, indicating that all suspects were in custody and that Operation Slaughter was ten-five. A sense of gratitude surged through Sebastián; knowing that Alex had come through safely amidst the turmoil eased the knot of anxiety that had settled in his stomach. The fact that there had been no reported casualties filled him with a profound sense of relief. At that moment, he realized just how fortunate they were, and he couldn't help but feel a spark of pride for the teamwork that had made this outcome possible. Sebastián, more importantly, began to reconsider his career and relationships with Alex and Leo.

As promised, Leo agreed to the paternity test, which proved that Landon Baxter was indeed Sebastián's father. Everyone, including Pa and Ma Franklin, were elated with the news. Sebastián and Alex began to gradually nurture their budding relationship, taking their time to explore the depth of their connection.

With an open heart and no expectations, Sebastián viewed this as an opportunity for a fresh start, free from the burdens of the past. He felt a profound sense of happiness that he had not experienced before, allowing the vulnerable boy within him to embrace the love and stability that comes from having two nurturing parents in his life. Together, they were creating a safe space where trust and affection could flourish, paving the way for a bright future filled with shared moments and deeper understanding.

Chapter 20

CLOSURE

After Royce left, Chris had the chance to converse deeply with Dominique and Lydia. Kane had revealed startling information about Bria's discoveries about the complex cartel operation. According to Kane, after Bria had left the state, she unearthed alarming details that suggested the cartel was not just involved in the transportation of drugs across various regions, including Arkansas, Tennessee, and Mexico, but that the operation extended internationally and deeply intersected with human trafficking.

Bria's findings were particularly concerning because they implicated multiple public officials, including several high-profile government figures, in this illicit trade. This revelation raised eyebrows about the extent of corruption and complicity in the cartel's activities.

On the critical night when Bria made the difficult decision to take her children to her parents for their safety, she had prepared to share crucial information. In a moment of trust and urgency, she had given Kane a carefully compiled list of names linked to the cartel, along with a thumb drive. This thumb drive contained a wealth of incriminating evidence and detailed accounts of the cartel's operations, which could potentially expose those involved and shed light on the system's dark nexus of crime and corruption. For Bria, this had not been merely a personal struggle but a courageous step toward unmasking a sinister network that extended far beyond her initial understanding.

Dominique was quiet during the conversation, and Chris questioned whether the uncovered information was critical for her. Lydia's report did not clarify its importance. However, it was noted that Nate had been arrested a few days before their meeting, which wasn't surprising given the intel Chris had received from Montana. Lydia and Chris scheduled a meeting for the following week to discuss a custody agreement that Bria's parents had requested.

Dominique had left shortly after Royce, so Chris did not have a chance to speak with her privately. Though she was no longer obligated to talk to him, Chris chose to give her a call. To his surprise, Dominique responded on the first ring.

"This is Dominique Sanchez."

Chris did not know if she had looked at her caller ID before answering or if she was trying to give him a taste of his own medicine.

"Ms. Sanchez, this is Chris Calloway. Are you still in the vicinity of Lydia's office?"

"I am not. I'm on my way to get dinner," Dominique replied. "Would you mind if I joined you?" he asked her.

"No, not at all. We can meet at the bistro in twenty minutes." "Okay, I will be there shortly," Chris said before hanging up.

When he arrived, the parking lot was packed. He should not have been surprised; it was a Friday night, and the band would be playing. His first thought was to call Dominique, but he knew she would not hear her phone ring.

Chris scanned the restaurant and spotted her at the bar, studying the menu.

From his previous dining experience with her, he knew better than to approach her while she was reading, especially if there was anything in her hands or on the table. She began conversing with the bartender, giving him the perfect opportunity to approach her cautiously.

Dominique saw him approaching and removed her belongings from the chair beside her.

He smiled at her as he sat down. "Good evening, Ms. Sanchez. Thank you for allowing me to join you."

"No problem. What did you want to talk to me about? The meeting, I assume?"

Chris cleared his throat. "No . . . I would like to talk about you." Dominique gave him a sharp glance and said, "What about me?"

"Why are you doing pro bono work for human trafficking victims who happen to be from Cuba or Puerto Rico?" He paused. "Did you know you had a twin brother named Dominic?"

Dominique sighed, crossing her arms as she sat back in her chair. "Well, Counselor, I see you came prepared with questions. Let's revisit the night we met here. After I left, I was followed by two black SUVs. I noticed they had been tailing me for a couple days. They cut me off that night at a traffic light about a mile from here. One of the occupants was Kane Gregory. Let's just say I'm the reason Nate didn't attend our meeting today.

"I knew I had another sibling, but he wasn't a twin. Dominic is a girl, and she was named after our father. After he was killed, my mother couldn't take us all on the boat that fled Cuba together, so my aunt agreed to take Dominic. That boat was said to have ended up in Puerto Rico, but no records exist of its arrival. I've spent the last two decades searching for her and my aunt. I went as far as traveling to both Cuba and Puerto Rico with no success. During my search, I uncovered that human trafficking had been linked to the boat that had carried my sister and aunt.

"So I appreciate Kane's information; it's the most credible I've received in the past five years. He also provided me with some valuable connections that I'm pursuing."

Dominique and Chris talked until the bistro's doors closed. Chris realized that he had judged Dominique and had made unfair assumptions about her. They vowed to work together and be advocates for educating the public on human trafficking.

* * *

Chris decided to drive to Nashville the next day and utilize his complimentary stay at the cozy Winston Inn and Suites. After yesterday's meeting, he felt a growing need to step away from his daily routine and allow himself some quiet time to reflect on his life and his complicated relationship with his father.

The weight of his parents' advancing ages loomed over him, poignantly reminding him that time was fleeting. Chris recognized that he could no longer afford to remain stagnant in cultivating meaningful personal connections and pursuing professional fulfillment. With a sense of purpose guiding him, Chris hoped this trip would help him reconnect with his aspirations and family.

Chris checked into his suite, then drove to his favorite burger spot: The Den. He was happy to see Fritz when he entered, and to his surprise, Fritz's mom was also there. He had the honor of conversing with Mrs. Ruby as he ate her famous burger. Her words touched Chris's heart; he knew this trip had been needed. Mrs. Ruby excused herself just as Chris Calloway Sr. approached the table.

Chris stood and greeted his father with a hug. He knew this was the beginning of a new chapter in his life, and he was ready to put pen to paper.

Chapter 21

CHANGING COURSE

Anya woke up with a renewed sense of purpose and determination coursing through her veins. It was a feeling she wished she had experienced two months ago when her choices seemed to spiral out of control. However, she was resolute in her mission to rectify her past mistakes.

She had spoken to Terri and was informed that Dela Cruz Investments and Jacob Realty and Investment Corporation had bought the buildings for the above-asked price. Anya remembered that Bryce was friends with the owner of Dela Cruz Investments and had also recently formed a partnership with them. Despite the complicated web of connections, Anya was determined not to drag Bryce into her predicament. She took a deep breath and picked up the phone to schedule a meeting with Mr. Dela Cruz. However, her heart sank when she was informed that he was out of the office and wouldn't return for several weeks. This setback did not deter Anya—instead, it prompted her to make the necessary adjustments to her plans.

In a determined effort to move forward, she decided to meet with one of the other agents at the firm. She made an appointment over the phone, securing a slot for one o'clock that afternoon. Not wanting to delay her progress, she also contacted Jacob Realty and managed to schedule a conference call with them later that day at four o'clock.

With her appointments confirmed, Anya understood the importance of being well-informed before her meetings. She instinctively turned to her laptop and launched a comprehensive search on Dela Cruz Investments and Jacob Realty. She delved into their histories, current projects, and any recent news that might give her an edge during her conversations. Anya knew that knowledge was power, and she was determined to be prepared when she stepped into the meeting rooms later that day.

Satisfied with her progress, Anya took a shower and called Royce again, but he didn't answer. She couldn't blame him if he didn't want to talk to her.

Just as she was getting ready to speak with the Dela Cruz agent, Leah called. "Hi, Leah," Anya answered. "Is everything okay?"

"Yes, I wanted to check in with you this morning. After we spoke last night, I wanted to ensure all was well."

"I am doing well. I forgot to mention that I ran into Grayson. He and his girlfriend were staying here, and I believe they left this morning for their cruise. I know our encounter was not a coincidence. I needed to see him and close a chapter in my life that was holding me back—it is *time* to move on.

"But enough about me! How are you and Bryce doing?"

Leah laughed. "We're still figuring out how to navigate this new, exciting phase of our lives. I just returned home on Monday from a trip to Mississippi, where Bryce and I celebrated my dad's birthday. Let me tell you, these hormones have me feeling like I'm living in two separate worlds!"

"Leah, you're *pregnant*, and those wild hormonal swings are totally normal. You're in your second trimester now, so hopefully you'll soon feel like yourself again."

"Me too," Leah said. "I can't continue seeing my man crash on the couch for the entire pregnancy!"

Chuckling, Anya said, "I suggest you and Bryce get a pregnancy massage together, or perhaps take a weekend getaway."

"That sounds like a great idea. When will you be back? And have you spoken to Royce?"

"No, not yet, and I wouldn't blame him if he doesn't want to. He gave me my space, so I must do the same. I hope to be back home by midweek. I need to go. I have a call with the realtor in ten minutes, but I'll call you later."

Anya whispered a quick prayer before joining the meeting. She realized her life in Miami wouldn't feel complete without Royce and Mia. If that meant putting this project on hold or having someone else manage the office, she was ready to do it.

* * *

Later, after wrapping up her meetings with both companies, Anya felt confident that she had made a positive impression. Soon after speaking with the

Jacob Realty agent, she received a call from Salvatore Dela Cruz.

"Good evening, Ms. McMichael. I hope I didn't catch you at a bad time."

Anya was shocked. She had not expected the company's owner to personally call her, especially since he was out of town.

"Good evening, Mr. Dela Cruz. No, this is perfect timing," she told him. "I'm reaching out to discuss your keen interest in our recently acquired

property located in the vibrant Arts District. Your exceptional appreciation for architecture, particularly your preference for designs that emphasize clean lines and elegance, caught my attention. My assistant was genuinely impressed by your depth of knowledge about our company and its mission.

"Additionally, your understanding of our contributions to the community strongly aligns with our values and goals. A conversation on this topic could yield fruitful ideas for collaboration or further exploration and purchase of the property."

"Mr. Dela Cruz, thank you for taking the time away from your vacation to speak with me. The first time that I viewed the property, I fell in love with it. It was as if it were talking to me. I would love to speak with you about future collaborations and finalizing the property purchase."

"I will have my attorney send the purchase agreement on Monday for you to review. I will also have Jaz schedule a follow-up meeting with you and our community liaison, who can connect you with people in the area. Welcome to Miami!"

"Thank you, Mr. Dela Cruz. Enjoy the rest of your time away."

Anya was over the moon, but her excitement was short-lived because she still had not spoken to Royce. Although she felt it was over, she would not give up until she had done everything possible to salvage their relationship.

* * *

On Monday, Anya received the purchase agreement from Mr. Dela Cruz, as promised. Upon reviewing the document, she noted that the asking price was lower than the initial proposal, which was a pleasant surprise. This new price fit comfortably within her financial plans and was beneath her original maximum budget, giving her a sense of relief and excitement. After careful consideration, Anya accepted the asking price and communicated her agreement to Mr. Dela

Cruz. She then sent the signed contract to the mortgage company to begin the final approval process, eagerly awaiting their response so she could move forward with her plans.

Anya called Leah and Abbey to share the news. When Leah asked if she had informed Royce, Anya started crying before answering. It felt like all she did was cry. Her professional life was flourishing, but her personal life was falling apart— and it was all her doing. After speaking with Leah and Abbey for an hour, Anya felt exhausted and sensed a migraine coming on. The past week's events had been overwhelming, and she knew she needed to rest.

Chapter 22

PLUS TWO

Royce had spent the night poring over the results, going through them a hundred times as if rereading might yield a different conclusion. As he finally drifted off to sleep that morning, his mind was still tangled in the implications of yesterday's news. The weight of the information pressed heavily on his chest, and he struggled to fully grasp its significance. Despite his excitement, he had not contacted anyone about Mia and Myles. The secret felt too fragile to share, wrapped in uncertainty and complex emotions, leaving him isolated in his thoughts. His children no longer had a mother and had a father who was foreign to them.

Kane had called and explained that Bria had bravely given the children to their parents to keep them safe. He said she had called the next day as she was on her way to the airport to board a flight to the States when she was involved in a crossfire between two road rage drivers, killing her instantly. Kane had alluded to Bria's death being suspicious and felt that Lucas, Nate, or Desmond might have been involved.

Anya had reached out multiple times, but Royce was trapped in a fog of thoughts and emotions, far removed from a mental state where he could converse with her. At some point he would talk with her.

Kane had also texted pictures of the twins; they were a blend of him and Bria. They both had sandy brown hair with blonde streaks at the tips. Myles's complexion was mocha, while Mia's was caramel, like Bria's. They both had striking grey eyes, which Royce learned that their maternal grandmother had, just like Kane.

Staring at the photos, Royce realized he was the father of two beautiful babies. He had no time to wallow in self-pity. These children depended on him, and so had Bria. Although their conception had not been planned, they would certainly be loved. Royce had less than two weeks to transform his bachelor pad into a kid-friendly home.

Royce contacted his interior designer, clearly articulating his vision for the space he wanted to create. He described the atmosphere he envisioned, including the colors, themes, and overall aesthetic. He trusted her expertise and allowed her the creative freedom to interpret his ideas and bring them to life.

Once the design plan was established, Royce took the next step by selecting and ordering all the essential furnishings for the space. This included carefully chosen beds that matched the style and comfort level he aimed for, playful and engaging toys that would inspire creativity, books to encourage a love for reading, and clothing for Mia and Myles.

Royce now felt he was in a good mental state to tell his family about the twins. He knew he would need their support when they arrived. He also considered calling Anya, who had reached out several times over the past five days. Her last voicemail suggested that she had been crying. After making the necessary calls to his parents and Logan, Royce spoke with Bryce and asked that he not share the information with Leah, knowing she would tell Anya.

Before dialing Anya's number, Royce mentally prepared himself. He did not want to cloud his perspective of what had happened over the past two months. He kept his conversations with Bryce and his mother at the forefront of his mind.

Who had inquired about Anya's thoughts and position on becoming a mother to children who were not biologically hers?

Royce was fully aware that Anya's answer would dictate the trajectory of their relationship, as his children came first now. He rehearsed what he wanted to say before he finally dialed her number. The phone rang twice before Anya answered. She sounded as if he had awakened her from a deep sleep.

"Hello, Anya, it's Royce."

"Hi, Royce," she mumbled, almost incoherently.

"Is this a good time?" He could hardly understand her.

"I was lying down. I have a migraine coming on. Can we talk in the morning? I took some medication, and it makes me sleepy."

"Sure, I will call you tomorrow."

"Okay. I love you and always will, Royce."

Hearing Anya say she loved him resonated in his spirit, unlike ever before.

Royce attributed it to their time apart. He had to consider what Bryce had said:

Love doesn't require us to be perfect but to listen.

* * *

As the first rays of sunshine streamed through her bedroom window, Anya awoke, feeling invigorated. She stretched beneath her warm blanket, excited to embrace another day. Then, she vaguely remembered her brief conversation with Royce the night before. The migraine medicine she had taken had wiped her out. Pausing to gather her thoughts, she pondered whether to call or text Royce first since he had said he would call her this morning.

"I do not have time to make this trivial," Anya said aloud. This was her life, and it may be the last opportunity to speak her truth. Dialing Royce's number, Anya paced the floor in anticipation. She was in the living room by now, looking out at the city. Imagining her and Royce walking hand in hand on the beach as they watched Mia running ahead of them.

"Good morning," Royce said.

Anya's mind drifted back to when she had heard his baritone voice for the first time. The vibration that erupted from her phone took her breath away.

"Is this a good time to talk?" she asked. "Yes," Royce answered. "What time is it?"

When she glanced at the time on her cell phone, it read 6:58 a.m. "Oh gosh, I had no idea it was that early," Anya said.

"No worries, you know that I'm an early riser. I have to run some errands this morning."

"I'm sorry I couldn't talk last night due to my migraine."

"I understand. How have you been these last two months?" Royce asked.

Their conversation began with dancing around the issue at hand, keeping it safe and mundane. Neither Royce nor Anya could express the true intent behind the call. It felt like they were both stuck in a cycle of courteous exchanges, unable to address the underlying tension that bubbled beneath the surface.

Royce's phone pinged, reminding him of his meeting with Chris and Lydia about the custody agreement for the twins. He needed to cut to the chase.

"Let's be honest, Anya. This conversation should've been done in person, and is damn, for sure, why we are separated. The issue is the absence of meaningful communication between us, and I can take responsibility for that. It also revolves around my deep desire to uncover the truth about Mia, whether she is my daughter, and how much Bria would be involved in our lives. I ask that you put yourself in my shoes for just one second."

Anya listened without interruption as Royce spelled out their current situation.

"Royce, I take responsibility for not being honest with you about my feelings and the impact Bria would have on our relationship. I understand that all of this happened before we were together. I wanted to be the one to carry your child, but I quickly realized that was not possible. Even though you always expressed how much you loved me, I felt trapped in that dim elevator, reliving the assault and its aftermath. A pregnancy. A pregnancy that I terminated out of fear of not knowing who the father was. Several months later, a blood clot traveled to my fallopian tube, causing it to rupture and leaving me with only a fifty percent chance of having a child. I was being selfish and didn't consider your feelings. I allowed my personal traumas to cloud my judgment. Royce Blackmon, I love you and vow to love Mia as if she were my own. But I understand if our time has ended and you have moved on."

After several moments of silence, Royce responded. "Mia is my daughter, but I also have a son—her twin brother Myles. As their father, and only parent, they are my top priority now. I *want* you to be part of our lives, but this is a package deal and you need to be sure. These children deserve someone who will be a constant presence in their life, just like me." Royce paused. "I know this is a lot to take in. And if you're not ready for this instant family, I understand entirely. I still love you, Anya McMichael, and no one else will love you as I do."

Anya held back the tears threatening to choke her. It *was* a lot to take in, but she felt ready and certain when she said, "I am here if you allow me to be."

"Would it be possible for me to call you back? Someone is at the door," Royce asked, catching Anya off guard.

"Sure," she answered, feeling perplexed as to why he had not acknowledged what she had said.

* * *

Several hours later, Anya was still feeling perplexed and slightly hurt. She was tempted to call Royce back but knew she needed to be patient and let him process everything they had discussed. This applied to Anya as well. There were two babies—*twins*. And based on what Royce had said, he was their only parent. Was Anya to assume that Bria was no longer in their lives, at least for now, or permanently? She did not want to take anything out of context.

Anya's phone rang, and she answered immediately, hoping it was Royce. Unfortunately, it wasn't. It was Hans informing her that her portrait had been delivered and that the courier would be coming up shortly with it.

When she heard the elevator doors sliding open, Anya called out to let the courier know she was busy in the kitchen. The room was filled with the aroma of spices and freshly chopped vegetables. As the courier entered, Anya's gaze was drawn to the large portrait he carried. It was so massive that it completely obscured his face, transforming him into a shadowy figure behind the canvas. Anya directed him to carefully lean the heavy frame against the back of the sofa, then she turned back to the stove.

A deep, familiar voice said, "This conversation needed to be finished in person."

Anya spun around, shock written all over her face. Royce stood before her, and this time she could not hold back the tears.

That evening, Anya and Royce talked about their expectations and future as a couple, ensuring they remained honest with each other, even when it was uncomfortable.

Love doesn't require you to be perfect but to listen.

EPILOGUE

One year later . . .

After overcoming several unexpected setbacks, the satellite office finally opened its doors in Miami. This marked not just a professional milestone but also a new chapter in the lives of Royce and Anya, especially as they embraced the joys and challenges of parenthood with their three-year-old twins, Mia and Myles. The little ones quickly became the heart and soul of their family, bringing laughter and chaos into every corner of their lives.

Their journey toward this so-called "happily ever after" was anything but smooth. It was marked by a series of tumultuous moments, each a test of their bond. From unexpected challenges like family crises to the everyday stresses that come with life, they faced obstacles that often left them feeling vulnerable and strained. Arguments erupted over seemingly trivial matters, and misunderstandings frequently clouded their communication. Yet through each storm, they learned more about themselves and each other, slowly building a deeper understanding and resilience that would ultimately strengthen their relationship.

The Blackmons were looking forward to the next chapter in their lives.

PREVIEW of Book 5 UNMASK: ROAD TO REDEMPTION

Sal is a devoted family man, deeply rooted in his commitment to those he loves. When his cousin Lou reaches out in distress, seeking help to find her long-lost parents, he feels an overwhelming urge to assist her. This search isn't just a routine favor; it stirs up buried secrets and unresolved issues from the past that challenge Sal's understanding of what family truly means.

As he dives deeper into uncovering Lou's family history, he questions the very bonds he has always cherished. Meanwhile, a chance encounter with the charismatic realtor, A.J., introduces him to the allure of a different life. Will A.J.'s charm and free-spirited nature entice Sal to abandon his wild ways in favor of a more settled existence?

Abbey, a young woman in search of the profound love her parents shared, feels the burden of high expectations. Her journey leads her to Jamerson Fischer, a man who appears to embody everything she desires in a partner. However, beneath her conscious feelings lies a secret admiration from another—an unrecognized attraction that could complicate Abbey's quest for true love. Will that admirer confront his feelings, or will his pursuit of the ideal relationship obscure his judgment?

Leah and Bryce are navigating the exciting yet daunting news of impending parenthood. The announcement of their little one could easily become overwhelming, testing the strength of their relationship. While friends around them struggle to maintain their connections under growing pressures, Leah and Bryce must decide whether this new chapter will bring them closer together or cause them to stumble. Will they rise to the occasion, working harder than ever to keep their love strong, or will the challenges of upcoming parenthood prove too significant for their relationship to withstand?

What road will these couples take?

PROLOGUE

Sal was very impressed with Ms. McMichael's portfolio and was excited that Jaz had contacted him after their meeting. He had Jaz send the paperwork to legal for review and requested they deliver the documents to Ms. McMichael by Monday at the latest.

Last night he had dreamt of A.J. again, and he could vividly see her outfit: a white asymmetric long-sleeve tunic, boot-cut jeans with rips at the knees, and white platform sneakers. Her hair was pulled into a ponytail that complemented her toffee skin tone, and she wore no makeup. He thought she was a natural beauty and planned to contact her once he returned home.

The next day, Sal was returning to the house alone because Matteo had an important business meeting to attend. He stopped at the local hardware store and purchased replacement locks, a surveillance camera, tools, and a ladder. Sal had noticed that several lights were out throughout the house and needed to be replaced.

Sal had spoken to Wynston last night, and she advised that the PI had sent her photos of a woman leaving the residence who resembled Selena, but he was not sure it was her because she wore sunglasses and a hat. Sal asked that those photos be sent to him.

As Sal opened the front door to the house, he noticed the light was on in the primary bedroom, and the shower was running. Sal quickly and quietly proceeded to the kitchen and removed a knife from the drawer. He walked swiftly to the bedroom, not realizing what he would find on the other side of the door when he opened it.

As Sal slowly turned the doorknob, the faint sound of running water grew louder, piquing his curiosity. Stepping inside, he saw a figure silhouetted behind the frosted glass of the shower door. The steam swirled around them, creating a misty veil that obscured their features, but the outline suggested a person lost in their world, unaware of his presence. Water cascaded down, glistening off their skin, creating a serene yet intimate atmosphere that left him momentarily speechless.

IllustrationBy Anthony J. Wardrett

Not every action requires a reaction—just wait on the outcome.

Dr. C.